THE TERRIBLE TWO

MAC BARNETT

TERRI
TW

Illustrated by KEVIN CORNELL

WELCOME TO YAWNEE VALLEY, an idyllic place with rolling green hills that slope down to creeks, and cows as far as the eye can see. There's one now.

Some facts about Yawnee Valley: If you placed all of Yawnee Valley's cows in a stack, they would extend to the moon and back. (But this is probably not a good idea since cows are afraid of heights and cannot breathe in space without helmets.)

In 1836, due to a balloting error, a cow was elected mayor of Yawnee Valley. (After earning record-high approval ratings, the cow was reelected to a second term.) A statue of that cow still stands in the center of the town square.

If you stand next to a cow for a whole day, you will hear that cow moo one hundred times or less. Counting moos is a popular pastime in Yawnee Valley.

That's one!

All this makes Yawnee Valley a very exciting place if you're enthusiastic about cows.

Miles Murphy was not enthusiastic about cows.

THIS IS MILES MURPHY. He's on his way to Yawnee Valley. Let's take a closer look at his face.

Notice the scowl. Notice the gloom. Notice the way his face is pressed against the window and he looks like he's trying to escape.

Notice the way he keeps sighing.

That's one hundred sighs today.

"Miles, please stop sighing," Judy Murphy said from the driver's seat. "We're going to have a house now! Your room will be bigger. And you'll have a yard! We'll have a fresh start. So a smile would be nice."

But Miles could not smile, because he was unhappy about moving to Yawnee Valley. He was unhappy about saying good-bye to his friends Carl and Ben. He was unhappy about saying good-bye to his old apartment in a pink building that was close to the ocean. He was unhappy about saying good-bye to his old bedroom, whose four walls and ceiling were plastered with maps that he'd tried to take with him but were plastered so well they tore when he pulled them down. (He shouldn't have plastered those maps so well.) He was unhappy about saying good-bye to Max's Market, his trusted candy supplier. And he was unhappy about saying good-bye to his reputation as his school's biggest prankster, which he'd earned through years of hard work and brilliant thinking.

Miles kept hoping they'd turn back and head home. But the car just kept going and was even now passing this sign:

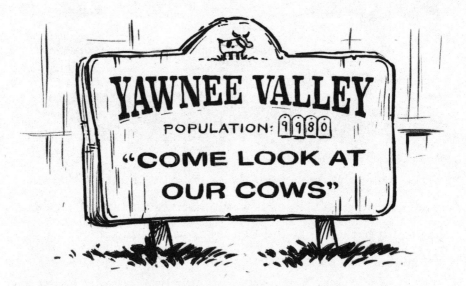

IT WAS WELL PAST MIDNIGHT, and Miles paced around his new bedroom. It was too big. The walls were too white. There were boxes everywhere. He should have been asleep, but he was awake, because this room was all wrong. And the house was all wrong. And the yard was all wrong. Miles didn't care about big rooms or houses or yards. This wasn't a fresh start. It was a rotten start. He turned off the lamp that sat on a box and got back in bed.

Miles couldn't sleep. Through the window of his old room, Miles would listen to the sound of waves crashing as he drifted off to slumber.

Miles got out of bed and opened the window. Somewhere in the distance, a cow mooed.

The air outside his old room smelled like the sea. This air smelled like cows.

Today was a bad day, but tomorrow would be an even worse day. Tomorrow he was starting his new school.

Miles went to bed with a sense of dread.

MILES AWOKE WITH A SENSE OF DREAD.

He opened his eyes and stared at his blank ceiling. Last night he'd dreamed it had all been a dream, and now he wished he were still dreaming.

Miles shut his eyes tight. He tried to fall back asleep, but downstairs he could hear his mother shuffling around the kitchen, preparing breakfast. Breakfast smelled like eggs. And cows. Although that might've just been the cows.

Miles ate his eggs. They tasted like dread, although that might've just been the dread.

The dread stayed with him on the car ride to Yawnee Valley Science and Letters Academy.

"Mom, what if I skipped this grade?" Miles said. "Lots of kids skip a grade. Then I could just spend this year working on projects. You know I have a lot of projects. This could be my project year!"

"Miles, when you skip a grade, you don't get a year off. You just start the next grade."

"I know that, Mom. But if I did that, I'd be younger than all the rest of the kids. That wouldn't be good for my development. That's why I think my project year is such a good idea."

"You're not having a project year."

"Maybe I could take this year to travel. You know I've been wanting to see the world! They say traveling is the best education."

"No."

"Maybe I could take a sabbatical. Do you know what a sabbatical is, Mom?"

"Yes. Do *you* know what a sabbatical is?"

"It's basically a project year."

"No."

They pulled up to the front of the school.

"Did you remember everything?" Judy asked. Miles checked around him. He had his new backpack, his new lunch bag containing his lunch, his new binder, his new folders, his new jacket, and—most importantly—his old pranking notebook.

It was a boring-looking notebook on the outside, of course (so as not to seem suspicious), but inside, it was a fabulous notebook filled with blueprints and maps and notes and plans for all the best pranks Miles had pulled.

The Ghost Prank. The Missing Front Tooth Prank. Operation: Soggy Homework. They were all in there, plus others. Two Cats Instead of a Dog. Fish in the Bed. Lemonade Without Any Sugar. Mission: Pie. Inside was all the great stuff that had made Miles famous. Ketchup That Looks like Blood. Raisins Everywhere. Operation: Sandy Shorts.

On your first day at a new school in a new town, you got to decide what kind of kid you were going to be. You could be the smart kid, or the kid who has cool shoes. You could be the kid who knows everything about old cars, or current events, or World War I. The kid who always has ChapStick. Chess kid, basketball kid, student-government kid. Kid who organizes canned-food drives. Front-row kid. Back-row kid. Kid who always has his hand up even though he doesn't know the answers. Kid who's allowed to see R-rated movies. Kid who isn't allowed to see R-rated movies but says he does and just makes up their plots based on the previews. Kid whose family doesn't own a TV and just wants to watch *your* TV. On the first day of school you could fake a French accent and be the foreign kid. You could bring your teacher a gift and be the kiss-up kid. Expensive-school-supplies kid. Kid who sharpens his pencil ten times per period. The two-different-socks quirky kid. The kid who wears shorts every day regardless of the weather. Today was the day when you could decide to become a new kid and be that kid for the rest of your life.

YAWNEE VALLEY SCIENCE AND LETTERS ACADEMY

PRINCIPAL BARKIN SEZ:

WELCOME BACK, BOVINES!

LET'S MAKE THIS OUR BEST YEAR!!!

But Miles didn't want to be any of those kids. He didn't want to be a new kind of kid at all. Miles wanted to be the same kind of kid he was at his old school: the prankster. Miles had been the best prankster his old school had ever seen, and he'd be the best prankster at his new school too.

"Bye, Mom."

He got out of the car and surveyed Yawnee Valley Science and Letters Academy. It was a squat brick building in the shape of a squat brick. Miles looked around and saw all the typical school stuff.

There was the typical marquee.

There was the typical flag attached to the typical flagpole.

There was the typical gaggle of kids.

The typical hedges.

The typical trees.

The typical school entrance blocked by somebody's typical car.

Wait. That couldn't be right. Miles looked again.

He approached the crowd of kids. Miles heard snickers. He heard snorts. He even heard some guffaws.

"There's a CAR on the STEPS," one kid said, stating the obvious.

"WHAT is going ON?" said the same kid. "I mean, SERI-OUSLY. Can somebody TELL ME?"

This kid was named Stuart. Anyone could have told him what was going on, but nobody did. (That sort of thing happened a lot to Stuart.)

Miles's heart was beating fast.

The bell rang, setting off the car alarm.

Nobody moved.

"I mean, HOW are we supposed to get into SCHOOL with THAT CAR there?" Stuart collapsed into hysterical tears.

Miles smiled for the first time since leaving his old town. That was a pretty good prank.

Then he stopped smiling.

It was a *very* good prank.

He frowned.

It appeared this school already had a prankster. A very good prankster.

Miles Murphy didn't know anything about World War I, and his socks matched. If Miles wasn't the school prankster, he was nobody.

PRINCIPAL BARKIN WAS SOMEBODY.

Principal Barkin was a principal. Principal Barkin was the principal of Yawnee Valley Science and Letters Academy, and at that moment, staring at a yellow car perched atop a flight of steps, he was an angry man.

At an earlier moment, Principal Barkin had been a happy man. That moment was 4:44 A.M., when Principal Barkin woke up one minute before his alarm went off. It was the first day of school, and nobody in the entire town of Yawnee Valley was happier.

He jumped out of bed.

First up was his shower: He spent two minutes shampooing, five minutes conditioning, and two minutes on a new song that he made up about school.

"Goodness gracious, here comes school / School, school, school, school, school, school."

Next, he picked out his favorite tie. (It took him one minute.) The tie was bright red with absolutely no pattern. The problem

with the tie was that it had a small mustard stain, but the good thing about the tie was that its color (the red of the tie and not the yellow of the mustard stain) was the color that conveyed absolute power. Always wear red. Presidents knew it. Bankers knew it. And Barkin knew it.

He ate breakfast: oatmeal on toast, a dish his great-grandfather had invented and deemed "The Breakfast of Barkins." This gave him exactly six minutes to reread his favorite chapter of his favorite book, *The 7 Principles of Principal Power*.

Principal Barkin got into his hatchback, sank into the leather interior, and drove to work in the dark.

He was the first person to pull into the lot behind the school that morning, just like every other morning, and he parked in the special "Principal Only" spot, which he had marked with a sign he'd made himself.

Principal Barkin got out of his car and buffed a smudge on his window with the back of his tie. He looked at the building, exhaled proudly, and walked in through the school's rear entrance.

Principal Barkin arrived in his office and settled into his chair. He cracked his knuckles. He sharpened a pencil. Then he hunched over a crisp sheet of paper and began crafting his First-Day-of-School Morning-Announcement Power Speech.

"I'm Principal Barkin, and I am your principal" he wrote and then crossed out. It was hard writing a power speech. He was a little rusty, and a good power speech required perfect concentration. At 6:15 the phone rang. Barkin picked it up and barked a gruff "Yes?"

"Howdy! I'm callin' from Armadillo Statio-

nery, in Amarillo, Texas. How we doin'? So listen: I'm callin' to offer y'all a great deal on paper clips and other office supplies, like staples! You like staples, pardner?"

"Not now!" Barkin hollered. "I'm writing a power speech!"

Principal Barkin slammed down the receiver.

At 6:21, the phone rang again. Principal Barkin picked it up, upside down, and yelled, "What?" into the wrong end of the phone. Then he turned it over and yelled, "What?" into the right end of the phone.

"Hello, good sir." This time it was somebody with a chipper English accent. "How are your windows this morning? Clean? I'm calling from the Laramie Cleaning Supply Company with a great offer on glass cleaner."

"I have no time for this now!" said Barkin. "Power speech!"

"You're probably wondering how an Englishman ended up in Wyoming selling janitorial supplies. It's an interesting story—"

"Call later!"

Barkin slammed down the phone.

At 6:36, the phone rang again. Barkin stood up. He knew what he had to do.

All principals should have a place in their schools that only they know about, where they can retreat to think and plan and write power speeches undisturbed. Principal Barkin was headed to just such a place, a secret place where he alone was king—his castle, his barony, his hidden land of hopes and dreams: the utility closet on the second floor.

Inside, Barkin moved a mop and pulled a chain to turn on the light. There was another mop in the way. He moved that mop too and sat down on a bucket. There, he began to write. Barkin, inspired, lost track of time as he wrote his speech. It took an hour. At 7:38 he emerged from the supply closet clutching perhaps the greatest first-day power speech in the history of Yawnee Valley Science and Letters Academy, at which point a student in the hallway told him his car was parked in front of the school entrance.

FORTY THINGS HAPPENED NEXT.

1. Principal Barkin threw his speech up in the air.
2. He ran downstairs.
3. He stood behind the school's glass doors, staring despondently at his car.
4. He noticed a number of students already milling about on the lawn.
5. He checked his watch. The bell would ring in nineteen minutes.
6. "Think!" he thought.
7. Principal Barkin fumbled for his car keys and dropped them on the floor.
8. He picked up the car keys.
9. Principal Barkin exited the school and crawled over the hood of his car.
10. He unlocked the driver's side door and got in.
11. The car's engine started.

12. Barkin put the car into drive.

13. He realized he could not drive his car down a
    flight of stairs.

14. The car's engine stopped.

15. "Think!" he thought.

16. He started up the car again and put it in reverse.

17. He slammed on the brakes.

18. "Stairs!" Principal Barkin reminded himself.

19. He crawled back over the hood.

20. Principal Barkin again stood at the doors of
    the school, wondering what to do next.

21. He ran to his office and dialed the Yawnee Valley
    Towing Service.

22. He asked the operator whether it was possible
    to tow a car down a flight of stairs.

23. The operator told him no.

24. He called the Yawnee Valley Police Station and
    asked the dispatcher if they could send a helicopter
    to airlift his car back into his parking spot.

25. The dispatcher told him no.

26. He slammed down the phone.

27. He picked it up again to make sure it was still working.

28. He ran back to the entrance.

29. He stared again at his beautiful car with the sun-yellow paint and the leather interior.

30. He checked his watch. The bell would ring in three minutes. "How will these kids get inside?" he asked himself.

31. He wondered whether he would have to cancel school. No principal had canceled school at Yawnee Valley Science and Letters Academy since the Blizzard of '32.

32. "There is a way," he thought.

33. "No," he thought.

34. "But I can't cancel school," he thought.

35. "But the leather interior," he thought.

36. The bell rang.

37. Principal Barkin knew what he had to do.

38. He opened the school's glass doors and stepped outside.

39. He climbed up onto the car's roof.

40. He cleared his throat and began to speak.

MILES MURPHY STOOD on the lawn of Yawnee Valley Science and Letters Academy, watching as a man climbed up on top of the car. The man cleared his throat and began to speak:

"Good morning, students. Who did this?"

Nobody spoke. Somewhere in the distance a cow mooed.

Principal Barkin had figured it wasn't going to be that easy.

"I see. Well, due to unfortunate circumstances, this morning, the first morning of what I hope will be Yawnee Valley Science and Letters Academy's best year yet, I will need all students, teachers, and staff to enter the school by first going through my car, being careful to mind the leather interior that I had

installed this summer as an early birthday present to myself—
my birthday is in three weeks, by the way, for anybody who
keeps track of those things and would like to show their appre-
ciation for their principal—but, yes, in any case, as I said, you
will be entering school through my car."

"But—" said a boy near Miles. Barkin eyed him.

"While I appreciate what I assume to be concern for my car's
leather interior, Mr. Jenkins, I have carefully considered the op-
tions, and this is the best available plan."

"But—" said a girl near the front of the crowd.

"I'm sorry, Miss Neeser, but if you or any of your classmates
think I am canceling school, you're sadly mistaken."

"But—"

"THERE IS NO OTHER PLAN!" shouted Barkin. "I
WILL NOW CLIMB DOWN FROM THE ROOF OF
MY CAR AND OPEN ITS DOORS. WHEN I BLOW
THIS WHISTLE YOU MAY CAREFULLY TRAVEL

THROUGH MY CAR AND TO YOUR CLASSROOMS. BUT BEFORE WE BEGIN OUR DAY, I JUST WANT TO ASSURE YOU THAT I WILL CATCH THE STUDENT OR STUDENTS WHO DID THIS, AND THE INVESTIGATION STARTS NOW, AS IN RIGHT NOW, BEFORE I EVEN BLOW THE WHISTLE! REMEMBER: I WILL BE WATCHING YOU, ALL OF YOU, AND I WILL NOT REST UNTIL I FIND THE CULPRIT. NOW, LET'S HAVE OUR BEST YEAR."

After Barkin blew his whistle, the students lined up single file to crawl through the principal's car. Principal Barkin watched, wincing. And flinching. And saying things like:

"THOSE SHOES LOOK MUDDY, MISS BERGNER!"

and "WHO TRACKED IN A LEAF?"

and "I HAD SOME PENNIES. WHERE'D MY PENNIES GO?"

Here's what Principal Barkin's car looked like when he drove it to school that morning:

And here's what Principal Barkin's car looked like when Miles Murphy, the second-to-last student to enter the car, finally got inside:

As Miles carefully contorted through the car, he heard the last student in line, a big kid who looked a lot like a small Principal Barkin, say, "But Dad—"

"WHAT IS IT, JOSH?"

"Why didn't you just have all of us go through the back entrance?" Then Josh muttered under his breath (but Miles heard him), "You nimbus."

It was true. The school did have a back entrance, and Barkin had walked through it this morning. (Please see page 18.)

Principal Barkin stared off at a field of cows in the distance. None of them mooed.

THERE WAS CHAOS IN THE HALLS.

"WHO WAS IT? WAS IT YOU?" Principal Barkin hollered to everybody and nobody as students streamed past. "OR WAS IT *YOU?*" None of the students were looking at Principal Barkin. They all knew better. Except for Miles, who had never seen an authority figure act quite like this. Actually, he'd never seen an authority figure *look* quite like this: Principal Barkin's face was so red that it was almost purple, like a grape, or a particularly nice sunset over the ocean back home. Miles's old principal used to get mad, but he never shouted. And he certainly never turned purple. This was mesmerizing.

"WAS IT YOU?" Principal Barkin stuck a finger in Miles's face. The finger was long and pale white, since most of the blood in Barkin's body was currently in his head.

"Huh?" Miles said. This was always a good thing to say when you might be in trouble.

"YOU. THIS IS MY SCHOOL, AND I'VE NEVER SEEN YOU BEFORE. WHY ARE YOU HERE?"

"I'm the new kid," said Miles.

Principal Barkin became slightly less purple.

"And what is your name, new kid?"

"Miles."

"Well, I don't like that at all," said Principal Barkin. "We already have a Niles at this school."

"My name is Miles."

"Well, that's better, but still a little confusing. Maybe you should go by Tony. Or Chuck."

"I'd rather go by my own name—Miles," said Miles.

"Well, you've got a little mouth on you, don't you? Which brings me back to my first question: WAS IT YOU?"

"Was it me what?"

"Was it you who moved my car to the top of the stairs?"

"No, sir. I don't even have a driver's license."

"And *that's* why you shouldn't have been driving my car. AS

WELL AS MANY OTHER REASONS."

"But I didn't drive it," said Miles.

"Then how did you get it to the top of the stairs?" said Barkin. "And how do I get it back down?"

"I don't know, sir."

Principal Barkin squinted. "Well, *Miles*, I'll have my eye on you. In fact, I'll have *both* my eyes on you. But in the meantime, welcome to Yawnee Valley Science and Letters Academy. How are you liking our town?"

"Oh, it's fine," said Miles.

"'Fine'? Only 'fine'? Yawnee Valley is a paradise! Grassy pastures and happy cows for miles, Miles. In fact, Yawnee Valley is the cow capital of the United States, this side of the Mississippi, excluding a couple of towns that cheat."

"I guess I'm just not very interested in cows," Miles said.

Principal Barkin turned a little bit more purple—orchid, perhaps.

Somewhere in the distance, a cow mooed. Principal Barkin pointed toward the mooing. Then he pointed at Miles.

"Not interested in cows?" said Principal Barkin. "NOT INTERESTED IN COWS?"

"Well," said Miles. "Um."

"Miles, if you are not interested in cows, it is simply because you are ignorant of the many reasons cows are interesting. Here, take this."

Principal Barkin reached into his Principal Pack, which non-principals called a fanny pack, and pulled out a booklet.

He thrust the book at Miles. "Take it. Read it. Love it. It is probably my favorite book, and not just because I wrote the foreword."

"Thanks," said Miles. "But I don't want to take your only copy."

"It's not my only copy. I've got a bunch more in my Principal Pack."

Miles wondered if he could go to class now. But Principal Barkin didn't move out of his way.

"Now, one last piece of business. All our new students get paired up with a buddy. Someone who knows the lay of the land, the school rules, what to do, what not to do, including moving my car. Since you are our only new student this year, you're lucky enough to have been assigned our best student. Niles!"

A small, blond boy wearing a sash that said SCHOOL HELPER ran over to the principal.

"Miles, this is Niles Sparks," Principal Barkin informed him. "Niles is the student who first told me about my car. Miles is the student who I suspect moved it."

Niles held out his hand, his elbow flexed just slightly, his eye contact with Miles uninterrupted by blinks. He was the kind of kid who practiced his handshake alone in his room. There was a Niles at every school. The kiss-up. The do-gooder. The school snitch. And now Miles was supposed to shake his hand?

"Sorry, I have a cold," Miles said.

Niles lowered his arm.

Principal Barkin frowned. "Well,

handshake or no, you two are school buddies. And a lucky thing for you, Miles. Niles is like a son to me. Of course, my own son also goes to this school and is also like a son to me."

Somewhere in the distance, a cow mooed.

"Niles," Principal Barkin said, "take Miles to Room 22. Ms. Shandy is waiting."

The two boys set off down the hallway.

"Nice sash," said Miles.

"Thanks!" said Niles.

FACT 1

A cow's normal, average body temperature is 101.5°F. That sounds like a bit of a fever! But it's not. It's their normal, average body temperature, as previously stated.

FACT 2

A dairy cow can produce more than 25 gallons of milk per day. That's 400 cups! Or 6,400 tablespoons! Or 19,200 teaspoons! But only 15,987 imperial teaspoons. Still, that's a lot of milk!

FACT 3

Cows have 360-degree panoramic vision. Want to sneak up on a cow? You can't. They see you.

WOW!

I HAVE TO ASK YOU SOMETHING," said Niles, "and I promise I won't tell Principal Barkin, but were you actually the one who parked his car in front of the school?"

"No," said Miles.

"OK, good," said Niles. "Because if you had I probably would have told Principal Barkin."

"Yeah," said Miles.

"I'm sorry I lied. But I think sometimes it's OK to do something wrong if it helps you do something right."

"Like ratting on me to Principal Barkin."

"Exactly! Principal Barkin relies on me to sniff out wrongdoers. Anyway, here's our classroom!" Niles opened a blue door. "There's Ms. Shandy's desk!"

"Is this the doorknob?" Miles asked, grabbing the doorknob.

"Yes! That's the doorknob!" said Niles.

Miles found an empty seat far away from Niles's.

Niles noticed. He got up and came across the room and sat in the seat in front of Miles.

"Buddy system!" Niles said, twisting around in his seat. "We have to sit by each other!"

"Great," Miles said.

The girl next to Miles laughed. "So, Niles is your buddy, huh?"

Niles answered for Miles. "Yes! I'm his buddy. Miles, this is Holly Rash. She's sitting next to you."

"Hi," said Holly. "What did you say your name was?"

"Actually, I was the one who said his name!" said Niles.

"I'm Miles," said Miles.

"Miles and Niles," said Holly. "That's confusing."

"No, it's not," said Miles and Niles at the same time. Miles gave Niles a dirty look. Niles gave Miles a really happy look.

"Well," said Holly, "if you're looking for any *real* information about this school, let me know."

Miles leaned over and whispered, "Who's the school prankster?"

"What?" Holly asked.

"Who put the principal's car on the front steps?"

"You mean it wasn't you?"

"No!" Miles said. "It wasn't."

"Yeah," Holly said. "I know. I was joking."

The bell rang. A split second before the trilling stopped, the big kid who looked like Principal Barkin burst through the door. He took a look at the teacher's desk and, discovering it was still empty, strolled down Miles's aisle. As the big kid passed Miles, he let his backpack hit Miles in the face.

"Watch it, nimbus," the big kid said to Miles. "Your face just hit my new backpack." The kid took a seat in the last row.

"So, who's he?" Miles asked.

"That's Josh Barkin, the principal's son," said Holly.

"That's Josh Barkin, the principal's son," said Niles.

"Josh is pretty much the worst kid in this school," said Holly.

"While I don't want to call anyone the worst, Josh is pretty mean sometimes," said Niles. "Also, he really likes the word 'nimbus' for some reason."

"Can I just hear from one of you," said Miles, "and could that one of you be her?"

Niles arranged his pencils on his desk into the shape of one big pencil.

Holly said, "Well, the deal with Josh is that he never breaks any rules at school, but still comes up with nasty tricks like hitting you in the face with his backpack. He never gets in trouble," said Holly, "but everyone knows he's a weasel."

"Still, he's our class president," said Niles, "and he's probably going to be our principal one day, so we should respect him."

"That guy is the class president?" Miles asked.

"Yep!" said Niles. "Just like Principal Barkin was always class president, and so was his father, and his father, and his father. 'The Barkins: from presidents to principals.' That's what Principal Barkin is always saying."

"But if everyone knows he's a weasel, why does he win?" Miles asked.

"He cheats," said Holly.

"Well, he used to run unopposed because he threatened to

beat up any other candidates," said Niles. "Technically, I don't think that's cheating. But for the last couple of years Holly has run against him and lost!"

"You lost to that guy?" Miles asked Holly.

"Twice!" said Niles.

"How?" Miles asked.

"The class president counts the votes," Holly said.

"That's a dumb rule," said Miles.

"The class president makes the rules," said Holly.

"That's ridiculous," said Miles. "If you know you're not going to win, why do you run?"

"I'm a protest candidate," said Holly. "My very presence in the race exposes the injustice of the system. Plus we get to miss class to write our speeches."

Miles was impressed.

"WHERE is the TEACHER?" asked Stuart, who was sitting to Miles's right. "I mean, the bell rang THREE MINUTES ago and there's NOBODY here. This is HILARIOUS."

Nobody laughed.

"Are WE supposed to TEACH OURSELVES?"

Just then, Ms. Shandy walked into the classroom.

"Sorry I'm late." Ms. Shandy tossed a canvas tote onto the big desk. "There was a car blocking the entrance and I had to go around the back."

"That car was CRAZY," Stuart said.

"Thank you, Stuart," said Ms. Shandy without looking up from filling out a seating chart. "I hope everybody likes where they're sitting. These will be your seats this year. Except for you, Josh. Why don't you move up from the back and take this desk in the front row?"

Josh looked mad for a split second, then grinned.

"Sure," he said. "I can move up to the front row. I'm not sure that my dad, Principal Barkin, would *want* me to move, though. He always tells me to be decisive, to make a decision and then stick with it no matter what."

"Move, Josh," Ms. Shandy said.

"OK, Ms. Shandy. I'm moving. Of course I'm going to listen to you. You're the teacher of this class, after all. However, I will be telling my dad that you made me move, even though I'd already found a seat in the back."

Ms. Shandy's smile tightened a little bit.

"NOW, Josh," Ms. Shandy said.

"But!" said Josh.

"No arguing."

"I'm *not* arguing!" Josh said. "But it might be worth mentioning that I'm the class president and so—"

"Josh."

Josh picked up his backpack. "You know, I could tell my dad you were late and you'd probably get fired. He's the principal."

"I know he is," said Ms. Shandy. Her smile tightened a little bit tighter.

"He's your *boss*."

Ms. Shandy turned to the board and began writing her name in big letters.

"For those of you who don't know me, my name is Ms. Shandy."

While Ms. Shandy was finishing up the "y" in "Shandy," Josh hit Miles in the head with his backpack on his way to the front of the class.

AT LUNCH, NILES SHOWED MILES the cafeteria.

"Here is where we get our trays," said Niles. "And there is where we get our food, from a lunch lady, which is a lady that serves our lunch."

"Right," said Miles. "I get it."

"And then over there are the tables. You might not know where to sit, since it's your first day, so you should probably sit with me."

Miles decided it was important to sit as far from Niles as possible.

Miles picked up a tray, which was soon loaded with turkey chili, tomato soup, macaroni and cheese, and a milk. Niles did the same.

"This all looks great, Mrs. Conlon!" Niles said to the lunch lady. "And I'd like for you to meet the newest student at Yawnee Valley Science and Letters Academy. His name is Miles."

The lunch lady looked around and then leaned in close.

"Well, a friend of Niles can have *two* milks." She placed another carton on Miles's tray.

Extra milk: the first good thing to come from being Niles's buddy.

Miles picked up his tray, turned around, and found himself face-to-face with Josh Barkin.

"My dad thinks you're the one who moved his car, nimbus," said Josh.

"OK," said Miles.

"That's going to be *my* car one day," said Josh.

"OK," said Miles.

"So basically you moved *my* car, you nimbus."

"But I didn't," said Miles.

"And you embarrassed my dad, and the Barkin family name, so basically you embarrassed *my* name. And that's why I'm going to beat you up. To preserve the honor of my name. And to avenge my future car. So I will probably beat you up twice— once for each."

"Well, I don't think your dad will like that," Miles said.

"Oh, I'm not going to beat you up at *school*," said Josh. "That would be against the rules, and I'm going to be principal here one day. But you know what, Miles Murphy? There's no school rule against beating you up on the sidewalk in front of your house, or behind the gas station, or in a pasture. I will think of other places too. Places where nobody will catch me. There are so many places where I can beat you up besides school, Miles Murphy. And nobody will ever know, except for me. And you."

There was only one thing to do.

Miles tilted his tray and spilled his lunch all over the front of his own clothes. Now he was covered in turkey chili, tomato soup, and macaroni and cheese.

"What the—" said Josh.

"Why did you do that?" Miles cried out. "Why did you do that to me?"

The kids in the cafeteria heard the commotion and turned to see Miles covered in food. They pointed. They laughed. The room went wild.

"What is going on here?" Ms. Shandy walked up to Miles and Josh. She stared at the stains on Miles's shirt.

"Josh came up and just knocked my lunch tray out of my hands," said Miles.

Ms. Shandy looked at Josh.

"I didn't!" said Josh. "That nimbus spilled it all over himself!"

"Why would I spill food on myself?" asked Miles.

"I don't know!" said Josh. "Because you're a maniac! Ms. Shandy, I never break the rules. You know that!"

Ms. Shandy looked from Miles to Josh.

"I think I can help, Ms. Shandy. I saw everything."

It was Niles.

"Thank you, Niles," Ms. Shandy said. "What happened here?"

"Yeah, Niles," said Josh. "What happened here?"

"Niles," said Miles.

"Josh walked right up to Miles and knocked the tray out of his hands," said Niles. "It was just like Miles said."

Josh was shocked.

Miles was shocked.

Ms. Shandy smiled. She had been waiting for this day for a long time. (Lots of teachers had.) "Come on, Mr. Barkin. We're going to see Principal Barkin." She led Josh out toward the principal's office. Everyone in the lunchroom watched them leave.

"Why'd you do that?" Miles asked.

"Josh made me swallow a rock over the summer. Twice."

"Well, thanks," said Miles.

"Here's your milks," said Niles, picking the cartons up off the floor. "They didn't break."

JUDY MURPHY FLOPPED A SLICE of eggplant onto Miles's plate. He hated eggplant, but tonight he wasn't even paying attention to food. Miles's mind was on other matters. Bigger matters. *Huge* matters.

"How was your day at school?"

"Fine," Miles told his mother.

◆ ◆ ◆

"How was your day at school?"

"Terrible," Principal Barkin told his wife. "Horrendous. Catastrophic. A complete and utter nightmare."

"I was asking Josh," said Mrs. Barkin.

"Oh," said Josh, fiddling with his steak. "Well, pretty much what Dad said."

"Oh dear," said Mrs. Barkin. "What went wrong?"

Principal and Josh Barkin said the same thing at the same time: "Miles Murphy."

"How's your homeroom teacher?" Miles's mother asked.

"Fine," Miles said, pushing eggplant around his plate.

"Her name is Ms. Shandy, right? What's she like? Is she nice?"

"She's fine," Miles said.

There were too many questions. Miles needed to focus. He was on to something, but his mom wouldn't stop interrogating him. Luckily, Miles had a trick for times like this.

"How was your day at *work*, Mom?" Miles asked.

"It was good, Miles, but I'd really like to hear about your—"

"Anything exciting happen?" Miles asked.

"No, nothing particularly exciting happened at work, honey," Miles's mother said.

"And what'd you have for lunch, Mom?" Miles asked.

"Lunch? Um . . . just a turkey sandwich and a small salad, dear. Now tell me about this Principal Barkin. I think I noticed him standing out on the lawn when I dropped you off. Did you get a chance to talk to him? Was he nice?"

The last thing Miles wanted to talk about was Principal Barkin.

"What were your *customers* like, Mom?" Miles asked.

If there was one subject that could set Miles's mom off, it was her customers. There were always so many of them, and they were always doing so many annoying things. Judy looked out the window and shook her head. Then she looked back at Miles. She sighed.

"I don't even know where to *start*," Miles's mother said. "Oh! I know! There *was* this one suit-wearing guy who insisted on cutting to the front of this *very* long line, and get this—he was on his *phone* the entire time. Right? So I said, 'Sir, if you don't mind, could you please return to your spot in line or maybe just consider taking your call outside?' And he was staring right at me, but I don't think he heard a *word* I said, Miles. In fact, I'm *sure* of it. So I repeated myself, asked him to return to his spot or go outside, but he just stood there, completely oblivious. So then . . ."

Miles smiled at his eggplant.

"Well, *I* certainly had an interesting day," said Mrs. Barkin. "When I was at the market—"

"I wasn't finished!" said Principal Barkin. "Don't you want to know how the car got off the stairs? I mean, when I left off, the car was still on the stairs! Aren't you wondering how Josh and I got home?"

"Oh," said Mrs. Barkin. "I hadn't thought of that, but I guess, yes, I do."

"So first I called a tow truck company and asked them if they could tow me down some stairs."

"What did they say?"

"I'm getting to that! They said no."

"Oh dear."

"Then I called the police and asked if they could send the helicopter over and lift my car off the stairs."

"What did they say?"

"Hold on, I'm about to tell you! They said no."

"Well, that's too bad."

"And then, finally, I had a brilliant idea. I called the junkyard, and I asked to talk to the magnet guy, you know, the guy who has that machine with the giant magnet that lifts cars off the ground and moves them all around?"

"Oh, what a fabulous idea, dear! What did he say?"

"He said no."

"Well, shucks."

"Let Dad finish, Mom."

"Sorry."

"And so, in the end, I just called Bob and asked him if he'd bring the forklift over from the farm and take the car off the stairs."

"That's wonderful! Why didn't you ask him first?"

"Because Bob has a big mouth! But I made him swear that he wouldn't tell Dad. Barkins' honor."

The phone rang, and Mrs. Barkin rose to get it.

"Who is it?" asked Principal Barkin.

"It's your father," said Mrs. Barkin. "He says he wants to scold you about the forklift, dear."

"How did he find out about that?" asked Principal Barkin.

"How did you find out about that?" asked Mrs. Barkin. "He says Bob told him."

"And that's how I met Deb, who seems just great," Miles's mother said. "I really think we're going to be good friends. She works at the post office too, one xwindow over from me. She was really helpful. I think we're going to grab dinner soon. She likes nature walks."

"That's good," Miles said.

"What about *you*, honey? Did you make any friends at school today?"

"No."

"No friends? Were there any nice kids? *Potential* friends?"

"Nope."

The phone rang.

"Hello. Yes? Yes it is. Oh, thank you. No, really, that's very kind. Well, you have a nice voice too. Of course, hold on, I'll get him."

"Who is it?" Miles asked.

"He says he's your new friend from school!"
Miles put his forehead on the table.

Principal Barkin put his forehead on the table.

Mrs. Barkin laid the phone down next to his ear.

"…COMPLETE AND UTTER DISGRACE. YOU ARE MAKING THE BARKINS A LAUGHINGSTOCK IN THIS COMMUNITY. DO YOU KNOW HOW LONG WE'VE BEEN PRINCIPALS HERE? THERE ARE FOUR GENERATIONS OF BARKIN PRINCIPALS, AND DO

YOU KNOW HOW MANY HAVE HAD THEIR CARS PARKED AT THE TOP OF A STAIRCASE?"

Principal Barkin was silent.

"DO YOU?"

"Zero?" said Principal Barkin.

"THAT'S RIGHT. ZERO. UNTIL TODAY. AND NOT A SINGLE ONE OF THEM, UNTIL TODAY, HAS HAD THE ENTIRE *SCHOOL* WALK THROUGH THEIR STUPID CAR TO GET TO CLASS. AND NOW I HAVE BOB TELLING ME HE HAD TO GET HIS FORKLIFT. YOU KNOW, IT MAKES ME THINK THAT MAYBE YOU HAVE A LITTLE TOO MUCH OF YOUR GRAND-FATHER JIMMY'S BLOOD RUNNING THROUGH YOU."

"Now, Father, I have never once canceled school, and—"

"IT MAKES ME THINK THAT MAYBE YOUR LIT-TLE BROTHER SHOULD HAVE BEEN THE PRIN-CIPAL AND YOU SHOULD HAVE BEEN THE ONE RUNNING A DAIRY. MAYBE BOB IS THE ONE MADE FROM REAL PRINCIPAL MATERIAL."

Principal Barkin groaned. "Well, I don't think that's true at all."

"Why not, Barry?" asked Bob Barkin.

"Bob?" said Principal Barkin. "Why are you on this call?"

"I PATCHED YOUR BROTHER IN WITH THREE-WAY CALLING!" shouted Principal Barkin's dad, Former Principal Barkin.

"Hey, bro," said Bob. "Sorry I told Dad, but, you know, he asked."

"So much for Barkins' honor," said Principal Barkin.

"YOU WANT TO TALK ABOUT BARKINS' HONOR?" said Former Principal Barkin. "TODAY YOU HAVE BESMIRCHED THE BARKIN HONOR. THIS IS THE WORST THING TO HAPPEN TO THE BARKIN NAME SINCE YOUR GRANDFATHER JIMMY—WELL, WE WON'T EVEN TALK ABOUT THAT. BUT WE WILL TALK ABOUT THIS: YOU HAD BETTER FIND THAT PRANKSTER, BARRY, AND MAKE AN EXAMPLE OF HIM."

"Yes, Dad," said Principal Barkin.

"GIVE JOSH AND SHARON MY LOVE."

Principal Barkin heard his dad hang up.

"How's your father?" asked Mrs. Barkin.

"I can't believe that little twerp Bob squealed on me," said Principal Barkin.

"Still here, Barry," said Bob Barkin.

Principal Barkin hung up his phone. His face was a deep indigo. "I will destroy Miles Murphy," he said.

◆ ◆ ◆

Judy Murphy put the phone next to Miles's ear.

"Hi, Miles!" said Niles. "It's me, Niles, your school buddy. From school. The one with the sash. We sat next to each other. All day today."

"Yeah, and then you followed me home," said Miles.

"Technically I was walking you home, except you were running, and I can't run very fast because of my allergies."

"OK," said Miles. "Why are you calling?"

"As your buddy I'm required to call you for a First-Day Check-In, which takes the form of a brief five-question survey."

"They make you call with a survey?"

"Yes!" said Niles. "Well, technically I created the rules for the school buddy program, so *I* make me call with a survey, but it should be quick and fun! You should be done before dinner."

"I'm eating dinner."

"Great! You should be back to dinner in no time!" said Niles. "Ready?"

"Shoot."

"Hold on a second, I have to put on my sash. You know, official business." There was rustling on the other end of the line. "All right. Question one. Please answer this: How great was your first day at Yawnee Valley Science and Letters Academy, on a scale of six to ten?"

"Um . . . a six?" Miles said.

"Great! A six! Next question: Do you foresee any school buddies turning into real buddies?"

"Um . . . honestly, I don't think so . . ."

"We can come back to that one. Question three: Did you park Principal Barkin's car at the top of the stairs?"

"Bye," said Miles.

"Wait! We didn't get to the essay questions!"

"Bye, Niles."

"Tell your mother I said bye!" said Niles.

Miles hung up the phone. He put his forehead back on the table. He closed his eyes.

For the sixty-seventh time today, Miles wished he'd parked the car at the top of the stairs. And for the seventy-third time, he wondered who did. If he didn't establish himself as this school's best prankster, Niles might actually end up being his real buddy.

Miles had to do something. Something big. Something huge.

"May I be excused?" he asked. Miles didn't even wait for an answer. He went right up to his room, pulled out his pranking notebook, and wrote:

THE INVITATIONS WENT OUT ten days later.

CONGRATULATIONS! YOU'RE INVITED TO

CODY BURR-TYLER'S THIRTEENTH BIRTHDAY PARTY!!!!!!!!!

THIS SATURDAY AT NOON ON THE YAWNEE VALLEY GREEN. (WE RENTED OUT THE GAZEBO.)

BRING PRESENTS

IMPORTANT: THIS INVITATION IS NOT A TICKET TO THE PARTY. YOUR TICKET IS A GOOD BIRTHDAY PRESENT.

ALSO, IT'S A POTLUCK SO DON'T FORGET TO BRING SOME FOOD AND DRINKS.

AND: I'M ONLY INVITING THE COOL KIDS, SO DON'T GO TELLING EVERYBODY. SHHH! SECRET. BE THERE OR BE LAME.

AND ALSO DON'T FORGET THE PRESENT. MAKE IT GOOD.

The hallway buzzed. Clusters of students huddled in corners, chattering. Some were looking over their shoulders. By the drinking fountain, Stuart was doing a little dance.

"Did ANYBODY ELSE get an INVITATION from CODY BURR-TYLER?"

Fourteen different students said "SHH!" at once.

Two girls were giggling near Miles's locker. He heard the shorter one say, "Yeah, I think he's the quarterback at St. Perpetua. He plays the electric guitar."

The taller one said, "Yeah! Cody Burr-Tyler is so cute!"

Miles smirked. Cody Burr-Tyler wasn't cute. Cody Burr-Tyler didn't even exist.

This morning was the culmination of more than a week's worth of planning that had taken up six full pages in Miles Murphy's pranking notebook. It was Miles's greatest achievement. Forget a car on some steps—Miles had invented an entire *person*: Cody Burr-Tyler, who'd be throwing the greatest birthday party Yawnee Valley had ever seen. He'd made up the invitations—only ten, because (and this was the masterstroke) you only needed ten, as long as you made the party a secret. Already kids were inviting one another. The invitations had only been circulating for eleven minutes, and this party was the social event of the season. At the party, Miles would reveal that there *was* no Cody Burr-Tyler—that the whole school had been pranked. And then (and this was the *other* masterstroke) he'd leave with all the presents everyone had brought. And everyone at Yawnee Valley Science and Letters Academy would know that Miles Murphy was the greatest prankster the school had ever seen. He'd be a legend again. An even bigger legend than he'd been in his old town. Nobody had ever pranked an entire school before. Miles folded his arms and leaned against the lockers. He pictured the glory. It was perfect.

"Good morning, buddy!"

Miles jumped. He turned around to Niles standing behind him. "Since we're school buddies and future life buddies, can I tell you a secret that I am not supposed to tell anybody?"

"Sure," said Miles.

"I mean, this is a big secret. I could get in trouble for telling you."

"OK," said Miles.

Niles leaned in close. "I got invited to Cody Burr-Tyler's birthday party."

"Who's Cody Burr-Tyler?" Miles asked.

"He's only the coolest guy in Yawnee Valley!" said Niles. "He plays football, he's in a band, ummm . . ." Niles looked down at the invitation. "He likes lightning."

"Wow," said Miles. "Sounds cool. Does he go to school here?"

"No. I think he must go to St. Perpetua. Anyway"—Niles looked both ways before continuing in a whisper—"do you want to come to the party with me?"

"I don't know," said Miles. "I wasn't invited."

"That's OK! Actually, technically it's *not* OK, because the invitation says that we aren't supposed to tell anyone, but, you know, like I said, sometimes it's OK to do something wrong if it helps you do something right."

"How is this doing something right?"

"Becoming party buddies!" said Niles. "Plus you're new, and it'll help introduce you to Yawnee Valley's vibrant social scene! Plus Cody Burr-Tyler gets more presents!"

Miles pretended to think it over.

"I'm in," he said.

"Great!" said Niles. "Here."

Niles handed over the invitation. Miles admired his own work.

The warning bell rang. A large reddish figure rounded the corner. Barkin.

"You! Tuck in that shirt!" Barkin yelled. "You! Spit out that gum! You! Stop doing that little dance! All of you! Stop huddling! Why are so many students huddling!"

Miles closed his locker and started down the hallway.

"You! Miles Murphy!"

Miles froze. "Yes, Principal Barkin?"

"Did you move my car to the top of the steps last week?"

Miles sighed.

"No."

"It would make your life a whole lot easier if you just admitted it now," said Principal Barkin. "Every day that you wait, the more trouble you— What's in your hand?"

Miles put the invitation behind his back. "Nothing, Principal Barkin."

"Well, now I know it's not nothing!" said Principal Barkin. "In fact, I know it's *something*! Something you don't want me to know about."

"It's just a piece of paper," said Miles.

"I *KNOW* IT'S A PIECE OF PAPER," said Principal Barkin. "I saw that right away. But now I know it's not just a piece of paper. I found that out when I asked you about it and you hid it right away. Yes! It's an old principal trick, Miles Murphy. Ask about something, and if a student hides that something, it's because he is up to something."

"Huh?" said Miles.

"Enough talking," said Barkin. "Hand it over."

Miles didn't move. This wasn't part of the plan.

"What is it?" said Barkin. "The plans to your next big prank?"

Miles tried to look calm.

"No," said Miles.

"Principal Barkin," said Niles, "it's just a party invitation!"

"A party invitation?" Principal Barkin's nostrils flared.

Niles put his hand over his mouth and directed a loud whisper toward Miles. "It's fine. Show it to him."

Miles had no choice now. He gave up the invitation.

Principal Barkin slowly put on a pair of reading glasses and peered at the paper. "Interesting. Very interesting. Cody Burr-Tyler, eh?" He snapped his gaze back to Miles. "Well, well, well," he said. "Well, well, well." Barkin folded the invitation and put it in his shirt pocket. "Well."

"Well?" said Miles.

Principal Barkin stared at Miles for four whole seconds. Then he pointed to a sign on the wall.

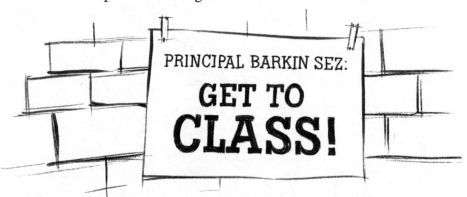

PRINCIPAL BARKIN SEZ:
GET TO
CLASS!

Miles exhaled. He turned, feeling flustered, and walked down the hallway in the wrong direction.

Niles called after him. "No, it's this way, Miles! We need to go this way!"

Miles turned around and followed Niles toward Room 22.

"Miles!" Principal Barkin shouted after him. "Remember: I'm on to you."

Barkin pointed at another sign on the wall. This sign hadn't been there yesterday.

PRINCIPAL BARKIN SEZ:
I'M ON TO YOU,
MILES MURPHY!

IT WAS INCREDIBLE. Miles didn't know the exact number of students at Yawnee Valley Science and Letters Academy, but he had a pretty good feeling that every single one of them was here for Cody Burr-Tyler's birthday party. The town square was packed with kids.

Two hours earlier, the place had been empty. Miles had arrived at 11:00 A.M., pulling a wagon behind him. He'd parked the wagon next to a picnic table next to the gazebo. On the table he'd taped a sign that said FOOD AND DRINKS HERE. Then he'd taped another piece of paper to the wagon: GIFTS HERE. Finally, he lifted the finishing touch from the wagon: a cake he'd made himself, from scratch, with pink frosting and HAPPY BIRTHDAY CODY BURR-TYLER written in fancy green lettering. (If Miles was going to prank everyone, it was only right to provide good cake.) Then Miles had left—he didn't want to be the first one at Cody Burr-Tyler's party. That definitely wouldn't be cool.

Now Miles had returned, and walked past a picnic table overflowing with food—brownies, chips, dip, cookies frosted pink and white with little sugar sprinkles on them; past three, no, make that four coolers full of soda and ice cream sandwiches; past his red wagon,

HAPPY BIRT
CODY

11

now filled with a tall stack of presents in colorful wrapping paper. There were red presents and blue presents and presents with balloons on the paper, which to be honest were a little babyish for Cody Burr-Tyler. Some boxes were flat. Some were round. One was pretty clearly a telescope. A telescope!

"I brought THAT ONE," Stuart said, pointing with both hands toward a small gift that seemed to be crawling away. "AW, MAN!" Stuart said, running after the box. "STAY!"

Miles made a mental note to leave Stuart's present in a pasture somewhere. He placed his gift—an empty shoe box in silver paper—on the wagon and grabbed a slice of cake. Two seventh-grade boys were standing by a platter of chimichangas.

"Have you said hi to Cody Burr-Tyler yet?" said the one wearing the red hat.

"Yeah," said the one not wearing any hat because he worried he didn't look good in hats. "I waved to him when

I got here. I don't know if he saw me—a bunch of guys were playing three flies up and Cody Burr-Tyler was permanent flier."

"Oh, that's cool. When I saw him he was telling this really funny joke about pizza. We did our secret handshake, and he said he'd talk to me later."

"Cool. You know, I think he *did* see me when I waved."

Miles grinned. Secret handshakes. Three flies up. They were doing his work for him.

Holly Rash was leaning against a tree. Miles walked up to her.

"Hey," said Miles.

"Hey," said Holly. "Look out for that cake. It's really dry."

"What!" said Miles. "I think it tastes good!"

"You're crazy. That cake is terrible."

"Maybe you just got a bad piece. Here, have a bite of mine."

"Never again," Holly said. "This is probably the worst cake I've ever eaten. And did you see that lettering? It looked like it said 'bird day.'"

"It says 'birthday'!"

"That cake is an embarrassment."

"Forget about the cake," said Miles. "What do you think of this party? Pretty great, right?"

"Eh, it's all right. To be honest, I was expecting more from Cody Burr-Tyler. I mean, I've never heard of the guy. But everybody talks about him like he's Cary Grant meets Marlon Brando meets Paul Newman."

"Who are they?" Miles asked.

Holly sighed. "Old movie stars."

"And . . . they all met?" said Miles.

Holly sighed again.

"What's a BIRD day?" Stuart shouted from over by the picnic table.

"This party really needs something to liven it up," said Holly.

"Hi, buddy, and hi, Holly!" A pair of tiny legs was the only thing visible behind a gigantic box that was waddling toward them. "It's me, Niles!"

"We know," said Miles and Holly at the same time.

"Oh! I wasn't sure you could see me behind this box."

They couldn't.

"That's some gift there, Niles," said Holly.

"Thanks! I hope I didn't go overboard. To be honest, it's not entirely safe. I can't really see when I'm carrying it, so I planned a route to the park that didn't involve crossing any streets. That's why I'm late!"

"What did you bring, Holly?" Miles asked.

"I brought myself," Holly said. "I'm not going to give a present to a guy I don't even know."

"What!" Niles's voice came from behind the present. "I went all out! I wanted to celebrate Cody Burr-Tyler for being born, and also thank him for recognizing that I was one of the cool kids by inviting me to this exclusive party."

Niles put down his box and for the first time saw the crowd that had taken over the town square. "Oh," he said. "Looks like someone shared the invitation."

Niles shrugged. "Oh well. More

gifts for Cody Burr-Tyler, I guess!" He adjusted his sash, which today said PARTY HELPER, and picked up his box. "I'm going to drop this off and then, cake time!"

Miles checked his watch: 1:26. Almost time for the big moment. He excused himself and set off looking for a quiet place to prepare. On his way to an empty playground, he passed two girls he'd never even seen before.

"Do you want the rest of my cake?" asked one girl.

"No," said the other. "I had some earlier and it was terrible."

"Do you think Cody is going to play his guitar today?"

"I hope so! Did you know Cody Burr-Tyler can crush a root beer can on his head?"

"Really?"

"Yep! With the root beer IN it."

"Whoa."

Miles loved it. This prank had taken on a life of its own.

And it was about to get better.

Miles made his way to a creaky swing set and pulled a crumpled paper from his jacket's inside pocket. It was his speech, which he'd written last night when he couldn't sleep.

The alarm on Miles's watch beeped. A cow mooed. Showtime.

Hello, everybody! My name is Miles Murphy, and I'm the new kid here in Yawnee Valley. I'd love to take this opportunity to say happy birthday to Cody Burr-Tyler. I'd love to, but I can't. Because Cody Burr-Tyler doesn't exist. I made him up! Yes, I'm sorry to say that this isn't a party celebrating Cody Burr-Tyler's thirteenth year. But it is a happy occasion: the greatest prank that Yawnee Valley has ever seen! [DESCEND GAZEBO STAIRS] Much better than a car on some steps. [GRAB WAGON HANDLE] And so there's nothing left to say but thanks for the gifts, and enjoy the cake. [EXEUNT WITH PRESENTS]

MILES STOOD NEXT TO THE WAGON full of
gifts. This was going to be good. He grabbed a fork and a
glass and dinged them together until he had the crowd's attention. Everybody turned to look at him.

"HEY, it's the NEW KID," Stuart said. "He's DINGING
that GLASS. Why is he DINGING a GLASS?"

With everybody's eyes on him, Miles ascended the gazebo's
five short steps. He took the speech from his pocket, cleared his
throat, and began:

"Hello, everybody! My name is Miles Murphy, and I'm the
new kid here in Yawnee Valley. I'd love to take this opportunity
to say happy birthday to Cody Burr-Tyler."

That's as far as he got before a yellow hatchback careened
into the parking lot, honking its horn. The driver's door flew
open and Principal Barkin spilled out. Purple faced and huffing,
Barkin hustled across the grass, waving his arms. "Stop everything!" he shouted. "Stop that kid!"

An uncomfortable murmur ran through the crowd.

"Miles Murphy!" said Barkin, arriving at the gazebo. "Stop this right now. You are done. Stand over there."

Miles walked down the gazebo's five short steps. The crowd gaped. Holly smirked. Niles nervously adjusted his sash. Barkin took the stage. "Students," he said. Principal Barkin stood in silence, waiting for everybody to stop talking.

When you are planning a prank it is important to plan for any contingency, and Miles had planned for this. In his pranking notebook, under the heading "POSSIBLE DISASTERS," Miles had listed "Thunderstorm," "Squirrel Attack," and "Busted by Grown-Ups." Miles knew, when Principal Barkin had confiscated his invitation, that there was a chance, however slim, that his prank would be compromised. And that's why he had an action plan for this moment: Sneak away with the presents. Miles gripped the wagon's handle.

"Students," said Principal Barkin. He removed a piece of paper from his pocket. What was it? A behavior report? An expulsion form? A warrant for the arrest of Miles Murphy?

No. It had guitars and footballs and lightning bolts. It was the invitation Principal Barkin had taken on Thursday. Barkin held it in the air.

"Students," said Barkin, "when Cody Burr-Tyler *personally* invited me to his birthday party, I was stunned. Although I probably shouldn't have been. Cody has always been the kind of upstanding lad who respects his elders. And although I am not even his principal—my understanding is that Cody goes to St. Perpetua, where he is a star on the field *and* in the classroom, not to mention his band, which, although I am not a big fan of contemporary music, well, even I can plainly see that Cody Burr-Tyler really rocks the house . . ."

As Barkin made a strumming motion with his hands, Miles began to realize something: He wasn't in trouble. The prank was still on. Miles stopped his retreat. He'd only made it a yard or so. He took his first breath in thirty seconds and looked at his principal.

"As I was saying, I assume Cody invited me because I am a pillar of Yawnee Valley. And that is why I'm here. To honor Cody and make sure that he is given a birthday speech by a pillar of the community, and not by some kid who just got here and is known to have some behavioral issues, like probably parking my car at the top of some steps."

Something hissed loudly.

"Sorry!" said Stuart. "That was my PRESENT!"

"Again, as I was saying, we are here for Cody Burr-Tyler's birthday. A very special birthday. His"—Barkin looked down at the invitation—"thirteenth. Wow. That's a big one. And that's why I pass on best birthday wishes from the whole Barkin family. My son, Josh, sends his regrets. He couldn't be here, because it's his mother's birthday. My wife also sends her regrets. She couldn't be here because it's *her* birthday. A lot of birthdays today! But I wasn't going to miss this party, which is of course the biggest of the year! And look at that cake! Can somebody grab me a piece?"

Niles rushed up to the gazebo with a giant corner slice.

"To Cody Burr-Tyler!" said Principal Barkin, his fork aloft.

"To Cody Burr-Tyler!" said the crowd.

"Happy birthday!" said Barkin through a mouth full of cake.

"Happy birthday!" said the crowd.

Principal Barkin smacked his lips a few times. "I'm sorry. This cake is a little dry. Could someone bring me a juice or something so I can give the rest of my speech?"

The crowd, tired of hearing Barkin speak, began chanting. "Cody! Cody! Cody! Cody!"

Barkin, overcome by the spirit of the crowd, his mouth still full of cake, joined in.

"CODY! CODY! CODY! CODY!"

Barkin clapped his hands and stepped down from the gazebo.

"CODY! CODY! CODY! CODY!"

All eyes were directed at the empty stage.

Miles smoothed the front of his shirt. The prank was back on. This was the moment. This was *his* moment. It was perfect. He walked back toward the gazebo.

The kids chanted.

The sun shone.

An electric-guitar riff blasted through the park.

The crowd parted, and from its midst arose a tall boy wearing a football helmet and jersey. He bounded past Miles and took the gazebo's five steps in a single leap. The boy had an electric guitar slung around his shoulder. The number on the back of his jersey was "1." The name was BURR-TYLER.

HELLLLOOOOOOOOOOOO, Yawnee Vallllllleeeyyyyy!"
the kid said. "Happy birthday to *me*!"

The electric-guitar riff sounded again.

Miles swayed slightly as his brain tried to process what was unfolding before him. Cody Burr-Tyler, a kid who didn't exist, a kid who Miles made up, was standing in front of him. And he was cool.

Although Miles's pranking notebook contained contingency plans for "Tornado," "Bird Attack," and "Food Poisoning," there was nothing in there for "Your Fictional Character Magically Becomes Real, Pulls a Green Pail Out from Behind the Gazebo, and Throws Footballs into the Crowd," which is what was happening right now.

The students made a frenzied scramble for the footballs, which Cody had autographed. Principal Barkin, being a good two feet taller than everyone else in the crowd, was catching most of the balls. He looked absolutely giddy.

"I'm open! I'm open!" he shouted.

Cody Burr-Tyler held the bucket upside down to show it was empty. The kids groaned and settled down.

"Hey! All right! That was a lot of fun! But if I could get serious for a moment—" Cody's voice got quiet. "I just want to thank you for making my birthday party exactly what I wanted it to be: the party of the year. Principal Barkin, thanks for that moving speech. I wish you were *my* principal."

Barkin applauded, alone.

"And to all of you, I just have one thing to say: Party down, live large, and thanks for all the presents."

The electric guitar started up again. Where was the guitar even coming from? Cody hadn't played the one on his back this whole time.

Cody Burr-Tyler gave a massive thumbs-up to the crowd. They roared. He jumped the banister and landed on the grass. Everybody roared again.

"Peace out, everybody!"

Cody Burr-Tyler took the wagon's handle from Miles. "Thanks for keeping this warm for me, little guy," he said.

Miles watched as Cody Burr-Tyler sauntered off with the gifts and loaded them into the trunk of a stretch limo, which apparently had pulled up during his speech. "Keep the party going without me, everybody," he said. "I gotta run. There's another party for me at my house."

Then Cody Burr-Tyler got into the backseat, still wearing his helmet, and the limo drove away.

WHAT JUST HAPPENED?

Miles was now sitting on the bottom step of the gazebo.

Seriously: What just happened?

Miles sat and wondered. Kids laughed, music played, and Miles just sat. Stuart still seemed to be chasing something. Miles sat. Cars pulled up, parents waved to kids, and kids got into cars. The cars drove away, leaving behind clouds of dust. Miles sat. The stragglers took the last of the food—hot dogs and brownies, but not cake. There was still plenty of cake. Miles sat. Holly and Niles came over and talked to Miles. Miles talked back. But when they left, Miles could not remember what they'd said. It was all just noise. Everybody else left the park, but Miles still sat. Somewhere in the distance, a cow mooed. Miles sat. The sun set and the park lights blazed, the sprinklers came on, and Miles just sat.

About an hour after dusk Miles decided that was enough sitting. He stood up.

Miles felt like he had entered a new world. Now that a fake kid had become real, anything was possible. Maybe the gazebo would launch into space and Miles would colonize the Horsehead Nebula. Maybe lightning would strike that oak over there, crack it open, and gold coins would pour forth. Maybe a volcano would rise up from the field and lava would devour Yawnee Valley, but the eruption's blast would also propel Miles safely back to his old apartment in a pink building that was close to the ocean, with maps on the walls and on the ceiling, back to his old town where he was a master prankster and everyone knew it. Miles waited a few seconds for something to happen.

Nothing happened.

All that was left of Cody Burr-Tyler's party was a field full of trash and a platter full of cake. Miles grabbed a garbage bag. He ate a fingerful of frosting and then dumped the cake in the bag. He picked up paper plates and candy wrappers, soda bottles and cans, pizza crusts and stray potato chips. Miles was supposed to leave the park with a wagon's worth of presents, but all he had was a big bag of trash. He didn't even have the wagon anymore.

He'd had that wagon since he was six! Despite what everybody said, Miles was starting to think Cody Burr-Tyler wasn't that cool at all. Take away the football helmet and the electric guitar, and all you had was a wagon thief.

The trash bag slung over his shoulder, Miles took one last look at the park. Underneath the picnic table was something he'd somehow missed.

It was a present.

Miles dropped the trash bag and ran for the table. He got on all fours. The wet grass soaked his knees. Miles crawled under the table and picked up the gift. He looked around for Cody Burr-Tyler, who might at any moment pull up in his limo and claim this last present. But no—Miles was alone. There, under the table, he held the present in his lap. It was the size of a shoe box and its silver paper shimmered in the moonlight. Miles bit through the ribbon and ripped off the wrapping. It *was* a shoe box! The lid was taped on. Miles worked his index finger under the tape. He popped off the lid. Tissue paper! He peeled back the paper and peered inside.

There, in the box, lying as lifeless as a real dead chicken, was a rubber chicken. This was apparently someone's idea of a joke.

He grabbed the chicken by the legs, walked back to his trash bag, and tossed it in. The chicken landed belly-up on top of some hot wings.

There was a message written on the chicken's belly.

Miles reached into the bag and pulled out the chicken. The words were written in big block letters.

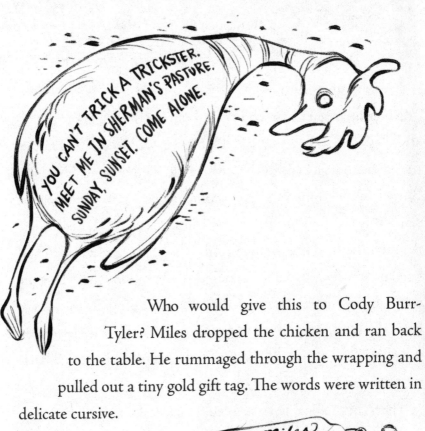

Who would give this to Cody Burr-Tyler? Miles dropped the chicken and ran back to the table. He rummaged through the wrapping and pulled out a tiny gold gift tag. The words were written in delicate cursive.

FACT

313

Cows have thirty-two teeth. Just like you and me!

FACT

314

Cows came to America with the Pilgrims—but they didn't wear those funny hats!

FACT

315

Cows can't vomit.

NEAT!

SUNDAY. SUNSET.

Miles clutched the chicken in his right hand, his grip firm. He transferred it to his left hand. Both palms were sweaty. So was the chicken.

Behind Miles was the sound of a breaking stick.

Miles whipped around.

It was Niles. Except Niles didn't look like Niles. It was hard to say what was different about him. He wasn't wearing his sash, but it was more than that. It was more than his mussed hair, more than his steely expression, more than his tan jacket and navy-blue turtleneck. Well, maybe it had something to do with the turtleneck. It was that Niles looked cool in the turtleneck, and Miles had never seen anybody look cool in a turtleneck. And Miles had never seen Niles look cool at all. But he did tonight. He looked taller. He looked . . . in control.

"Why did you bring the chicken?" asked Niles.

Miles looked down at the chicken, then back up at Niles.

"Um . . . I thought we might need it."

"For what?"

"Like, maybe this meeting had something to do with the chicken," said Miles.

"The chicken was just a way to deliver a message. A prankster often communicates with another prankster by writing a message on a rubber chicken."

"Oh," said Miles. "OK. So do you want the chicken back? Or should I just keep him, or drop him somewhere, or—"

"Forget about the chicken!" Niles said.

Somewhere in the distance, a cow mooed.

This meeting was getting away from Miles. "You ruined my birthday party prank!" he shouted at Niles.

"I saved your birthday party prank."

"Saved it? *Saved* it?" Miles tried to laugh, but his mouth was dry and he could only cough. "That's insane. You stole all my presents. Or Cody Burr-Tyler stole my presents. Or whoever that was. Who was that?"

"Some kid from Hillsdale I paid twenty bucks to impersonate Cody Burr-Tyler."

"And he has my presents?"

"Nope. I have your presents, Miles."

"And you call that saving my prank?"

"Your prank wasn't even a prank."

"What?"

"Let me ask you, Miles, how did you expect your 'prank' to play out?"

"I was going to get up there, tell everybody I'd pranked them, and get a bunch of presents."

"So you were just going to walk away with all those presents? After you told the entire school that you'd lied to them?"

Miles thought for a moment.

"Yes."

"How was that going to work, exactly?"

"I guess I thought they'd be so stunned by the prank that they'd just watch me go."

Niles stared at Miles.

"All right, I see your point," Miles said. "But it still would've made my name. I would've pranked the entire school in one go. Everybody would've known Miles Murphy."

"Yeah, Miles Murphy, the liar and thief."

"Well, when you put it that way . . ."

"If you prank everyone, who is left to appreciate the prank? Pranking everybody is like pranking nobody."

"Huh?" said Miles.

"You're forgetting one of the basic rules of pranking," Niles said. "The goat has to deserve it."

"The goat?"

Niles rolled his eyes. "Do your research, Miles! A goat is what pranksters call their victims. And to be a goat, someone has to have it coming. Everyone loves to see a goat get pranked. That's why Principal Barkin is a great goat. He always has it coming. Plus he turns purple."

"So you were the one who put Barkin's car at the top of the steps!"

Niles stared at Miles again.

"Who are you to lecture me about pranking?" Miles asked. "I was the best prankster at my old school! I was a legend!"

"You were a yak."

"What?"

Niles sighed. "A yak. A yak is someone who's always bragging about his pranks. A prankster doesn't prank for the fame. A prankster pranks for the prank."

Miles tightened his grip around the rubber chicken's neck.

"Listen," said Niles. "When people know you're a prankster, they're all watching you. Kids are waiting to see what you do next. Principals are tailing you down the halls. To a real prankster, that's death. The best pranks require a lot of work. They require preparation. To pull truly great pranks, you need to be invisible. The best pranks leave everyone wondering."

Niles had a point. If Miles was being honest, his classic Operation: Sandy Shorts would have been a much better prank if his homeroom teacher hadn't caught him immediately. And the stuff about goats made sense too. By the time Miles left his old town, Carl and Ben, his closest friends and near-constant pranking victims, weren't really taking his calls anymore. But. But! "But it's so fun taking credit for your pranks," Miles said.

Niles smiled. "I agree. That's why I sent you the chicken. That's why you're here today. I have a proposal."

Miles waited.

"I'm proposing," said Niles, "that we team up. We become a pranking duo. Co-conspirators. A secret society founded on mutual admiration and the joy of pranking. I even have a name picked out. We'll call ourselves the Terrible Two."

N O THANKS, " SAID MILES.

"What?" said Niles. It was the first time he'd looked uncertain today.

"I don't want to join your dumb society."

"But it would be good for you, Miles! I could teach you to avoid suspicion and—"

"You? You could teach me? You think you could teach me?" Miles's face was feeling hot. "I don't need you to teach me anything. I'm a pranking *legend*."

"Oh, I didn't mean to offend you," Niles said. "I agree: You have real potential."

"'Potential'? 'POTENTIAL'?" Miles was shouting now, but he didn't know it. "I have executed pranks you would never dream of. Ever hear of Situation: Cold Oatmeal? The Great Bifocal Caper? You're such a pranking expert—did you in your research ever come across a little prank called Pile of Potato Bugs?"

"I haven't heard of any of those pranks," Niles said.

"Then maybe you're the one who could learn from me. Because I invented them!"

"OK, OK," Niles said, holding out his hands. "Miles, I didn't mean to imply that—"

"You think I need you?"

"I think we could help each other."

"Ha, ha!" Miles said. (He actually said, "Ha, ha!")

Niles just stared, so Miles continued.

"Well, I'll say it again: No thanks. No thanks now and no thanks forever. I'm not going to be second banana on your little prank team. In fact . . ." Miles drew in a big breath. "I declare a prank war."

"Miles, I don't want—"

"You're scared! You're scared! The prank expert is scared."

"Let's not—"

"I'm not taking it back! It's war. It's a prank war."

"Miles, I seriously think you should seriously think about what you're saying."

"No, Niles, why don't you go seriously think. Go home and start thinking, start planning, real seriously. You're going to need every brain cell you own. Because you can think and think and think, but I'll always be right behind you, one step ahead of you."

"All right, then. If that's what you want. I'm sorry that—"

"Yeah, I'm sorry too, Niles. I'm sorry your little meeting didn't go as planned. You probably thought I was going to come here tonight and sign right up to be your stooge. But that's just it, Niles Sparks: You don't know me. You don't know what's going on up here." Miles tapped his head with the chicken's beak. "And that's why you will never win this prank war."

"Suit yourself," Niles said. "The prank war is on."

Miles Murphy watched as Niles walked away. He watched as, in the purple evening, Niles became a Niles-shaped silhouette among cow-shaped silhouettes. He watched so intently that he didn't notice Josh Barkin coming up behind him until he was already in a headlock.

"I *knew* you'd be here, nimbus," Josh said.

"How?" was all Miles could get out through his windpipe.

"That little nimbus Niles Sparks told me. He sold you out! He called me last night and said he'd tell me where you'd be if I agreed not to beat him up for lying about the lunch tray."

Miles would have sighed if he could have.

"Even your buddy isn't your friend!" Josh said. Then he punched Miles in the gut.

Miles dropped the chicken.

DAY ONE OF THE PRANK WAR," said a cool voice inside Miles's head as he hid behind a plant outside the teachers' lounge. "Or day two of the prank war, depending on whether you count that business last night with Josh Barkin, which I don't."

Miles checked his watch. Nine minutes. He had nine minutes to execute his opening salvo. Activity Time, between second and third periods, was a chance for students to grab a snack or step outside. It was fifteen minutes, bell to bell. Six of those minutes had been burned already, waiting for the corridor outside the teachers' lounge to clear. Now Miles was the only one left, peering out from behind a large philodendron. Since he'd taken his post at the beginning of

Activity Time, he'd counted eight teachers entering the lounge. That meant he needed eight teachers to leave, right now.

Miles unzipped his backpack and removed his pranking folder. The folder was nondescript and had the word FORMS written across it, which was the most boring word Miles could think of. Miles opened the folder and pulled out the thing that would empty that teachers' lounge:

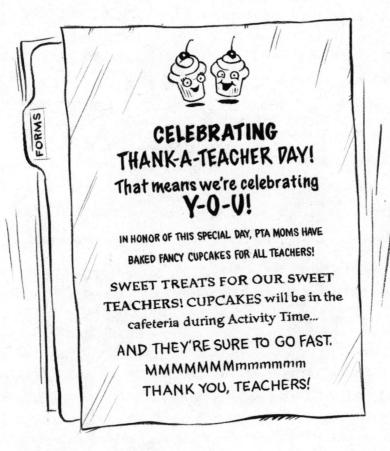

FORMS

CELEBRATING THANK-A-TEACHER DAY!
That means we're celebrating
Y-O-U!

IN HONOR OF THIS SPECIAL DAY, PTA MOMS HAVE BAKED FANCY CUPCAKES FOR ALL TEACHERS!

SWEET TREATS FOR OUR SWEET TEACHERS! CUPCAKES will be in the cafeteria during Activity Time...

AND THEY'RE SURE TO GO FAST. MMMMMMMmmmmmmm THANK YOU, TEACHERS!

Miles looked down the hallway in both directions. All clear. He did a little roll out from behind the plant, scrambled across the carpet, and slipped the bright-green flyer under the door. He knocked twice, jumped back behind the philodendron, and waited.

The second hand of Miles's watch ticked eighteen times before he heard the door open. Out came Mrs. Thoren, followed by Ms. Lewis, Mr. Gebott, Ms. Machle, Mrs. Trieber, Mr. Stevenson, and Mr. Maxwell—all on their way to a table in the cafeteria loaded with cupcakes (made with extra egg yolks, so they'd be extra moist, a recipe adjustment Miles had made after the whole dry-cake debacle at Cody Burr-Tyler's party).

"I like cupcakes," Mr. Maxwell said to Ms. Machle.

"I hope there's chocolate," Mrs. Trieber said to Mr. Stevenson.

"I don't get why they didn't just bring the cupcakes to the lounge," Ms. Lewis said to nobody.

That was only seven teachers. Miles needed eight. The door swung shut. He waited another full minute. And then another thirty seconds. Six and a half minutes to go. Who was left?

Miles tried to recall the procession into the lounge. It had all happened so fast. There were kids everywhere, Barkin was shouting somewhere in the distance. Clanging lockers. Swinging backpacks. A flash of silver track pants. Yes! It was Coach O.!

Miles was confused. Why hadn't Coach O. left? Coach O. had the look of a man who loved cupcakes. In fact, Miles had seen him eating prepackaged cupcakes every day for the first three weeks of school.

But only for the first three weeks.

Miles slumped against the wall as he remembered a conversation he'd overheard between Coach O. and Coach B. during P.E. last week: Coach O. was going low carb.

There were definitely carbs in cupcakes.

If Miles didn't think fast, the whole prank was shot. How could he get Coach O. to leave that lounge?

It was almost automatic: Miles pulled out his pranking folder, removed a blank sheet of bright-green copy paper, and began to write.

He gave the flyer a once-over and then applied the master-stroke: a smear of ink on the bottom right-hand corner that looked just like copy-machine toner.

ALSO THERE'S

BACON!!!

HAPPY THANK-A-TEACHER DAY!

Perfect. Roll. Scramble. Slide. Knock.

Miles was back behind the plant in less than six seconds. Coach O. was out the door in less than three more. The silver track pants swished down the hall and disappeared around the corner.

Three minutes left. This was it. For the last time, Miles left his cover and hurried across the hall. He grabbed the handle, paused a second, and pushed through into the teachers' lounge.

The teachers' lounge. Off-limits to all students. The sanctum sanctorum. It smelled like coffee.

Everything was beige except a dark-brown couch with a big white rip down the center cushion. There were mugs everywhere and months-old magazines and nearly finished crossword puzzles. At the center of the coffee table was a platter half full of doughnuts. And there, on the back wall, was a pigeonhole message box with three dozen little cubbies, most labeled with a last name. The teachers' mailboxes.

Every step Miles took across the room was imbued with the thrill of the forbidden. He felt like a spy in his enemy's castle. Miles wasn't even breathing as he stood in front of the mailboxes, scanning strips of tape scrawled with handwritten names. Alvarez, Andresen, Barkin.

Miles had practiced this next move the night before: Without looking he reached into his pranking folder, took out a long white envelope, and stood on his tiptoes. He took one last look at his forgery:

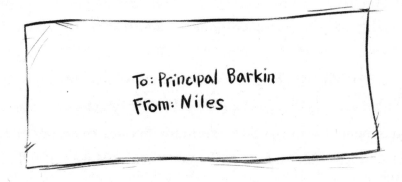

Miles chuckled, kissed the envelope, and plunked it into Barkin's box.

He grabbed a sprinkled doughnut on the way out the door. By the time the bell rang, he was in the main hall and the doughnut was in his belly.

A LL RIGHT, GENTLEMEN, ALL RIGHT! Come on,

line up, line up!" Coach O. was shouting between blows on his whistle. "Quit standing around in little clumps! You need to line up and stop clumping!"

Nobody lined up. Josh Barkin jumped up and touched the net of a basketball hoop while a few other boys watched. Stuart was wearing his shirt inside out. Two boys and a girl were reading on the bleachers. Somewhere outside the gymnasium, a cow mooed.

"Come on! Line up! Line up!" Coach O. was getting desperate. "Don't you guys know it's Thank-a-Teacher Day? Although, really, some thanks—there wasn't even any bacon. And I'd been told there'd be bacon."

"The cupcakes weren't that good, Tom," said Coach B. "They were dry."

Over by the trophy case, Miles rolled his eyes.

"Well, it certainly looked like you were enjoying them

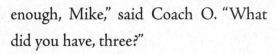
enough, Mike," said Coach O. "What did you have, three?"

"Nobody's keeping you from eating cupcakes but yourself, Tom," said Coach B.

"I'm low carb!" said Coach O. Then he started blowing his whistle again. "Line up!"

The many clumps gradually coalesced into one big clump.

"You call that a line? I call that a clump!" said Coach O.

"Or a blob," said Coach B.

After much shifting and shuffling and some shoving from Josh Barkin, the clump thinned out into a line.

"Now *there's* a line!" said Coach O.

"Good line," said Coach B.

Coach O. blew his whistle for no immediately identifiable reason. "We're starting a new unit today—indoor hockey. The

most important rule of indoor hockey is what? It's this: No. Swinging. Above. The knees."

"Keep those sticks low," said Coach B. Coach B.'s whistle was in his mouth and it blew faintly as he talked. "Swing those sticks high and you could accidentally hit someone in the face."

Josh looked at Miles and smiled.

"Now," said Coach O. "We've got sticks over there, pucks over there, and cones over there. Grab a stick, partner up, get a puck, and practice passing to each other. Then I'll tell you what to do with the cones. Go!" Coach O. blew his whistle and the line immediately dissolved back into clumps.

"These kids just don't listen," Coach O. said to Coach B. "It's making me nuts. Look at my hands shake."

"Tom, maybe you should eat some crackers or something."

"I can't eat crackers, Mike! Crackers aren't on the diet!"

"Stop shouting, Tom."

The coaches got deep into an argument punctuated by the occasional blasting of whistles at each other.

Miles watched as Niles dutifully plucked a rubber puck out of a mesh bag. Look at him, Miles thought. He almost felt bad for him. Poor Niles. Niles didn't even know what was coming. And what was coming was the thrilling conclusion to a devastating prank.

All day, Miles had been waiting for Barkin to show up, purple faced, and pull Niles out of class. It hadn't happened in science, or in history, or during silent reading. It hadn't happened in art class. And so it would have to happen now, in P.E., the last period of the day. And oh, how perfect! P.E., which meant that Niles would be called into Barkin's office wearing his gym clothes. How embarrassing! And then he'd get suspended. Or maybe even expelled! No matter what, Niles Sparks would be a goat. Because here is what Miles had placed in Principal Barkin's mailbox earlier that morning:

Dear Principal Barkin,
I, Miles, regret to inform you that on the first day of school I parked your car at the top of the stairs. This is my confession. I am sorry. I don't know why I did it but I understand you will probably have to punish me harshly. That's fine. I deserve it and I respect you.
— Sincerely Niles

Miles didn't know what Niles's signature looked like, and so his masterstroke was that illegible scrawl at the bottom of the paper. And now here was Niles, his size-small gym clothes at least two sizes too big, loping over with a plastic hockey stick under his arm.

"Want to partner up?" Niles asked.

Miles shrugged. "I don't have a stick."

"That wasn't what I meant. Have you given more thought to the pranking partnership?" Niles checked to make sure nobody was within earshot. "The Terrible Two?"

"Oh, that," said Miles. "What's the matter? Regretting starting this prank war with me?"

"You started the prank war."

"Whatever. You know what, Niles? It sounds to me like you're scared. It sounds like you're thinking it would be better to have me close instead of out in the wild, dreaming up stunning and masterful pranks."

Miles checked the door to the gym. Now would be the perfect time for Barkin to show up.

But Barkin didn't show up.

Instead, Niles reached into the pocket of his gym shorts and pulled out an envelope.

Not *an* envelope.

The envelope.

For the first time in today's P.E. class, Miles felt out of breath. "Where'd you get that?"

Niles gave a matter-of-fact shrug. "I sort and deliver Principal Barkin's mail—it's one of the duties of the School Helper. As you can probably imagine, I was surprised to find a letter from myself in Barkin's mailbox. So I steamed it open over the electric teakettle and found your confession."

"Amazing," Miles said, in spite of himself.

"That's what I'm trying to tell you, Miles! If you never yak and keep a low profile, you're above suspicion. And if you're above suspicion, you can get access to the inner workings of the whole school. I've worked my way into a place where I can execute spectacular pranks." He paused, then added, "And foil underwhelming almost-pranks."

"What do you mean 'almost-pranks'?"

"This wasn't a prank."

"Of course it was a prank!"

"No. This was just ratting me out for a prank I committed. That's not a prank. It's just a jerk move. And a violation of the Prankster's Oath."

"I've never heard of any Prankster's Oath."

"Of course you haven't," said Niles. "But if you join the Terrible Two—"

"Nope! No way. I'm not going to join your dumb club just to learn some phony oath you probably made up. I'm a born prankster! Prankster blood pumps through my prankster heart!"

Niles sighed. "So the war is still on?"

"The war is still on."

"OK." Niles held the envelope out in front of him. "Take a closer look."

To: Principal Barkin
From: Miles

"What!"

Miles grasped at the envelope, but Niles pulled it back.

"I took care of the inside too. Look."

Dear Principal Barkin,
I, Miles, regret to inform you that on the first day of school I parked your car at the top of the stairs. This is my confession. I am sorry. I don't know why I did it but I understand you will probably have to punish me harshly. That's fine. I deserve it and I respect you.
             — Sincerely Miles

"This could come in handy in the prank war," said Niles. "A signed confession, written in your own handwriting."

"That is not my handwriting!" Miles said. In fact, Miles had been very careful to disguise his handwriting—he'd closed his eyes while writing the note.

"It looks a lot more like yours than mine."

"How do you know?" Miles asked.

"The Third-Week Check-In I had you fill out," said Niles. He produced another piece of paper.

Please write a brief essay, in cursive, describing your experiences in the first three weeks at school, using comparisons from literature, history, and/or film/television.

Go suck an egg, Niles!
Sincerely, Miles

Looking at the evidence in front of him, Miles had to admit that the handwriting in the confession did look like a messier version of his own.

"Plus, I don't write with a blue Bic Velocity 1.6-millimeter ballpoint pen," Niles said. "But you do. In fact, you may remember that I borrowed yours in science. I used it to change the 'n's to 'm's."

Miles had to admit the kid had a knack for planning.

Niles put the confession back in the envelope, licked the flap, and sealed it shut. "I think I'll hold on to this," he said. "Just in case I need to put it back in Barkin's mailbox."

Miles gave Niles his best sneer. "Wouldn't that be ratting?" he asked. "Isn't that a violation of the Prankster's Oath?"

Niles smiled. "It would only be ratting if you'd figured out how to put Barkin's car at the top of a flight of steps," he said. "But you didn't dream up that stunning and masterful prank." He leaned in close. "*I did.*"

Niles turned and walked away. Coach O. and Coach B. were still blowing their whistles when the bell rang.

A dairy cow can produce 120 pounds of saliva per day. That's a lot of imperial teaspoons.

Cows can walk up stairs, but not down, because of the way their joints work. Sounds like the excuse my grandma gives! (Although my grandma can walk neither down nor up stairs.)

Cows are social creatures and prefer to form large herds, but will sometimes avoid certain cows. That's right: There are popular and unpopular cows.

SO COOL!

MS. SHANDY STOOD IN FRONT of the class wearing a long skirt and red sneakers. "Would anyone like to be the first to share their report?" she asked.

Niles Sparks raised his hand and kept it aloft, his elbow forming an almost perfect right angle—just like Miles knew he would.

Ms. Shandy paused to see whether any other students would volunteer.

Nobody did—just like Miles knew they wouldn't.

"OK, Niles, come on up."

Niles strode to the front of the room, carrying a black shoe box under his arm.

It was all going according to plan.

One thing Miles Murphy had reluctantly acknowledged after the Forged Confession Fiasco was this: If he wanted to out-prank Niles, he was going to have to get better at planning.

Handwriting, pen varieties, the mail-sorting responsibilities of the School Helper—Miles hadn't looked into any of these things. Miles admitted that, yes, he could learn from Niles Sparks. (It made him a little queasy to admit it.) And so he had embraced new tactics. He would be more alert, more patient, and above all, more prepared.

A couple of weeks after Niles had confronted him in P.E., Miles began brewing his next prank.

The scheme started to take shape in Ms. Shandy's social studies class. She'd assigned a one-page oral report on an ancient civilization. Niles had taken a quick look at the grading rubric before raising his hand.

"Ms. Shandy, may we use visual aids to enhance our presentations?"

"Sure, Niles, but I'm not giving extra credit."

"But we could use a visual aid if we simply thought it might supplement our own learning and the learning of the class?"

"Yep. That's fine."

"Yessssssssss," Niles whispered loudly.

"Let me guess," said Holly. "Diorama."

Niles didn't say anything, but he'd already begun sketching a rectangle on the back of his rubric.

＊ ＊ ＊

At lunch, Miles got the scoop from Holly.

"He does a diorama for *everything*. Last year he made like nine dioramas. In English we had to do book reports and he made a diorama of *Lord of the Flies*. It had a jungle with real moss and a light-up boar's head with little red eyes that flashed. In math we did a unit on three-dimensional shapes, and he brought in a rectangular solid that doubled as a diorama of the personal library of René Descartes. In science we had to do earthquake dioramas, and he did a diorama of a thrust fault plus a second diorama that was a making-of diorama of the original diorama."

"He really likes dioramas," Miles said.

"You think?" said Holly.

"Hey, Holly?" said Miles. This had been bugging him for a while. "Have you ever seen someone look cool in a turtleneck?"

"Sure. Steve McQueen. Richard Roundtree."

"Who are they?"

"Old movie stars." Holly sighed. "Hey, can I have your fruit snacks?"

Miles loved fruit snacks, but Holly had earned them today. Or at least half of them. This was good information.

"Hi, Holly. Hi, nimbus." Josh Barkin had sidled up to their table.

"Hi, Josh," said Holly.

Josh pulled out a chair and sat in it. "Holly, let's talk." He gave Holly the same smile he gave teachers. "As winter break approaches, I know we're all considering our political futures. I hope you're not planning on running for class president when we come back."

"I am."

"Well, I admire your optimism, Holly, I really do. But given that you've lost the last two years, I thought I'd offer you a place on my ticket. How would you like to be vice president of our class?"

"We don't have class vice presidents, Josh."

"I could talk to my dad about creating the position."

"I'm running for president, Josh."

"I'm sorry to hear that." Josh frowned. "And while of course I'd never beat up a girl, I will beat up your nimbus friend here if you run."

Holly shrugged. "Go for it."

Miles gave Holly a look like, *This is just a tactic, right?*

Holly gave Miles no look whatsoever.

Josh stood up, made sure nobody was watching, and kicked over the chair. "You guys are both nimbuses."

"Thanks a lot," said Miles after Josh was gone.

"He's already after you anyway," said Holly. "At least now you're a political hero."

She had a point.

"Welcome to the resistance," said Holly. "Here, have some fruit snacks."

Miles wanted to remind her that the fruit snacks were already his, but he figured she knew that.

The reports were due in two weeks. Never before had Miles's pranking journal been so full of diagrams, outlines, and questions.

By Friday he had the prank figured out.

Step one: Research. While changing for P.E., Miles had snuck a peek at Niles's school shoes. Shiny black wingtips: size 7. Write that down.

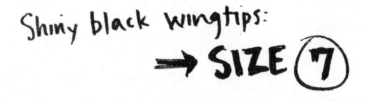

Step two: Lay the foundation. Step two began as soon as his mom picked him up from school.

"I need new school shoes," said Miles.

"You just got new shoes," said Judy Murphy.

"Not like *these* shoes. Nice shoes."

"Those are nice shoes."

"*Nice* shoes."

"Those are *nice* shoes."

"*Nice nice* shoes."

"Those are *nice nice* shoes."

This wasn't working. Change tack.

"Mom, it's just that . . . never mind."

"What?"

"No, I don't want to talk about it."

"Miles, you can tell me."

"Well, it's just that kids are making fun of these shoes."

"Bullies? Are they bullying you?"

"No, it's not like that—"

"Is there bullying going on at your school? Because I just watched an hour-long show about bullying and—"

"No, no. It's just—"

"Because you should not change who you are because of a bully. Look at me, Miles. Do not change you. Or your shoes. Now, if you want me to talk to Principal Barkin about setting up a zero-tolerance zone—"

This was going all wrong.

"Mom! I'm not being bullied. That's not even the main reason I wanted new shoes."

Come on, Miles.

"The main reason I wanted new shoes is . . . I think I need to stop dressing all sloppy. It's like you said when we were school shopping—it wouldn't hurt me to start dressing more like a young man sometimes."

By 4:22 P.M. Miles owned a pair of black wingtips just like Niles's. He hated them. But he was pretty excited about the box.

Step three: Commence construction. In the mornings, as soon as his mom's car was out of the parking lot, Miles untucked his shirt and changed into his sneakers. After school, he straightened his clothes and put the wingtips back on. And every night, he worked on his diorama.

First things first: Miles wore a 9. A little Wite-Out and a permanent marker fixed that quickly.

The rest of the diorama took a lot longer. Miles spent all week

cutting, drawing, gluing, sculpting. The work lasted through the weekend. Late Sunday night, he finished. Miles was too tired to admire his handiwork. Well past midnight, he dashed off a page about the Egyptian pharaohs and went to sleep.

On Monday morning Niles walked into Ms. Shandy's classroom carrying a black shoe box that, on the outside at least, looked just like the one in Miles's backpack. Niles took a seat and tucked the box neatly beneath his chair.

Inside, Miles was wild, sweaty, jittery. Outside, Miles was boring, normal, like a shoe box.

The bell rang, like it always did.

Ms. Shandy took roll, like she always did.

Niles got up and hung the attendance sheet on a hook outside the classroom door, like he always did.

And that's when Miles dropped his pen on the floor and, in one smooth motion, bent down, switched the two boxes, and retrieved his blue Bic Velocity 1.6-millimeter ballpoint.

Niles returned to his desk. He hadn't noticed a thing.

Miles stared down at his report and smiled as he pictured the mayhem that would ensue.

Because Niles had made a diorama of the Hanging Gardens of Babylon.

And Miles had switched it with a diorama of Principal Barkin taking a bubble bath.

Ms. Shandy stood in front of the class wearing a long skirt and red sneakers. "Would anyone like to be the first to share their report?" she asked.

Niles Sparks raised his hand and kept it aloft, his elbow forming an almost perfect right angle—just like Miles knew he would.

Ms. Shandy paused to see whether any other students would volunteer.

Nobody did—just like Miles knew they wouldn't.

"OK, Niles, come on up."

Niles strode to the front of the room, carrying a black shoe box under his arm.

He placed the shoe box on Ms. Shandy's desk. The top was still on. Niles loved a big reveal.

"I am here to show you one of the most beautiful sights in the world," Niles said.

Miles covered his mouth with a folder.

"A magnificent vision that, until today, has been obscured by the mists of history."

It was almost too perfect.

"Prepare yourselves. For we are journeying to a forbidden sanctuary that will surely amaze you."

Niles reached for the top of the shoe box.

"Behold!"

With a flourish, Niles Sparks removed the top and revealed a stunning replica of the Hanging Gardens of Babylon.

"Even I have to admit that's a pretty good diorama," Holly said.

"Ancient scholars attribute this wonderful Wonder of the Ancient World to King Nebuchadnezzar II," Niles went on, "although some historians believe the Hanging Gardens of Babylon weren't in Babylon at all, but belonged to the Assyrian king Sennacherib."

Impossible.

This was impossible.

Miles had switched the boxes. Hadn't he? He had. Right? Yes. But maybe he should double-check? He should double-check. Because if Niles still had the Babylon diorama, what was in his backpack?

Miles ducked under his desk. He opened the shoe box and released two thousand crickets into the classroom.

C RICKETS?" SAID PRINCIPAL BARKIN. He was leaning so far over his desk that his purple head hovered uncomfortably in what Miles considered his Personal Zone. "CRICKETS?"

"Yes," said Ms. Shandy, who was seated in a big chair next to Miles's big chair. "Crickets."

"Ms. Shandy, I was addressing Miles." Principal Barkin hovered. "CRICKETS?"

"Yes," said Miles. "Crickets."

"Miles Murphy, is this your idea"—Barkin's nose wrinkled and his tongue rested against his two front teeth—"of a prank?"

"No, sir."

A cloud of crickets erupting from a shoe box. Girls screaming. Boys screaming. Josh Barkin ducking under his desk like he was in an earthquake drill. Stuart standing on his chair and holding a leaf aloft, crying out, "It's OK, everybody! I have an IDEA!" Crickets leaping onto faces, into hair. Crickets bouncing off the walls. Stuart waving the leaf (where had he gotten that leaf?), shouting, "It's their FOOD!" The feeling of crickets on flesh. The noise—the collective chirping more like a constant screech, like a car spinning through an intersection. It was an amazing prank—but, no, sadly, no: It hadn't been Miles's idea.

"Then why, Miles Murphy, did you release a swarm of crickets into Ms. Shandy's classroom?"

"It was an accident?" said Miles.

"An accident."

Principal Barkin smirked the smirk of a principal who had a troublemaker cornered. "And why, Miles Murphy, were there thousands of crickets in your backpack?"

Miles winced the wince of a cornered troublemaker. As soon as the crickets had erupted from his backpack, Miles had known he'd have to answer this question. But he hadn't come up with an answer. What could he do, tell the truth? Of course not! Principal Barkin would never believe his own School Helper could be responsible for something like this. Niles was right: He was above suspicion. Plus, telling the truth would be ratting, and Miles wasn't a rat. And also the truth involved confessing to making a diorama of Principal Barkin taking a bubble bath, which seemed unwise. Miles was stuck and he knew it. What could he say? Why would he have thousands of crickets in his backpack?

"It was a visual aid," said Miles. "To enhance my presentation."

The color of Barkin's face seemed to flicker.

"A what?"

"Ms. Shandy said even though we wouldn't get extra credit, we could use visual aids if we thought they might supplement our own learning and the learning of the class."

"Is this true, Ms. Shandy?"

Ms. Shandy was giving Miles a strange look. "I did say that, yes."

"Well, in that case . . ." Barkin's face softened and took on the hue of a nectarine before going back to eggplant. "But wait! Miles Murphy, this is ridiculous! A visual aid is a diorama or something! How is a swarm of crickets supposed to supplement the learning of your class?"

"Well, my oral report was on the pharaohs of Egypt. These crickets were supposed to represent the plague of locusts. You know, from the Ten Plagues? Because as I'm sure you know, scientists and historians believe that the story of the ten plagues may have actually arisen from real natural disasters—"

"Of course I know that!" said Principal Barkin. "That's true, isn't it, Ms. Shandy?"

"Yes," said Ms. Shandy, still looking at Miles.

"Well," said Miles, "I wanted to show what a swarm of locusts would look like. Only, the crickets weren't supposed to get out." Miles put on his most sincere face and shrugged. "I guess I ended up doing a better job supplementing the class's learning about swarms than I'd even planned to." An innocent chuckle faded back into rueful earnestness. "I know *I* sure learned a lot."

Principal Barkin exhaled through his nose. He sat in his chair and slouched. "I don't know. Something smells bad."

"Probably the crickets," said Miles helpfully. "They kind of smelled like sweat."

"Not literally!" said Barkin. "Something smells bad metaphorically. And Barkins have great metaphorical noses. Something is *off* here, Miles Murphy. Something is wrong. This, Miles Murphy, is strike two."

"What was strike one?" Miles asked.

"Strike one was parking my car at the top of the steps, which I still don't know how you did."

"I didn't."

"Just as you say you didn't mean to release the crickets! And in this metaphor, saying you aren't responsible for a prank constitutes a strike! Strike three will be another prank that you deny committing, which will mean you have 'struck out,' which in this metaphor means that you will have actually done that prank and all the other pranks. So strike three makes the previous strikes real, in essence transforming them from denied pranks to—"

"Principal Barkin," said Ms. Shandy, "if that's all, I think Miles should probably get back to the classroom and start rounding up the crickets."

"Oh, yes, of course," said Barkin. "Ms. Shandy, if you'll remain here, there's something I'd like to discuss with you."

Miles stood up. Was this really it? Would he really be leaving unpunished?

"Why are you lollygagging?" Barkin shouted. "Go!"

Chapter 23

NILES SPARKS WAS WAITING on the other side of Barkin's door.

"You are one slippery customer," said Niles. "That visual-aid business was inspired."

"How'd you hear that?"

Niles produced a drinking glass from behind his back. "Old-fashioned listening device," he said.

"Does that really work?" Miles asked.

"Try it."

Miles held the tumbler up to the door and pressed his ear against the bottom.

"Yes, but I didn't cancel class," Ms. Shandy was saying. "I just had the students continue their presentations down on the lower field instead of in a classroom full of crickets."

"Yes, yes, I understand that," said Barkin. "It's just that you must know we Barkins are sensitive to even the *appearance* of an interruption in instruction. And I think you'll find I'm being very open-minded. I mean, if my father had seen your students all gathered under that oak tree in the middle of a school day!"

Miles handed back the glass. "Neat," he said, trying to not express how neat he actually found it.

The two boys headed down the hallway.

"This time you actually did come up with a really good prank," Niles said.

"Gee, thanks," said Miles.

"I mean it."

"How'd you know I was going to do it?"

Niles stopped.

"How'd you know I was going to switch the shoe boxes?" Miles asked.

"I saw you changing out of those wingtips in the parking lot before school all last week," said Niles. "It was pretty easy to figure out why you'd have a pair of shoes exactly like mine, if you didn't want to wear them. Although you should really give wing-

tips a chance. Once they're broken in, they actually conform to your foot and—"

"But how—"

"You took the crickets when you switched the shoe boxes. Then I swapped your diorama for mine while you weren't paying attention. What were you doing, just looking down at your desk? Let me guess: picturing me up there with that Barkin diorama?"

Miles didn't say anything.

"Something I've learned," said Niles. "You can't celebrate a prank before it's over."

Miles couldn't tell whether he was angrier at himself or at Niles. Probably Niles.

"Oh great. Expert advice from Dr. Expert." It wasn't a great line, but he was very angry.

"Miles, this is like a magician revealing the secrets behind his tricks. I'm only telling you this stuff because I respect your talent for improvisation. That's why the Terrible Two is a great—"

"Oh please. You know, Niles, it's easy to sit there and tear everything down. But it's another thing to actually *create* something."

"What?"

"Seems to me this prank war's been pretty one-sided. I keep coming up with pranks, you keep foiling them. Big deal. Why should I want to team up with you? Because you figured out how to park a car at the top of some steps once? Great. Ooooh. Wow. You've been playing defense for the last six weeks. If you're such a great prankster, then bring it."

"OK," Niles said, and walked off.

Miles went to clean up some crickets.

FACT 777

Average cows weigh about 1,400 pounds, and absolutely none of them feels self-conscious or weird about it!

FACT 778

Studies have shown that classical music helps cows produce more milk. So the next time you need milk from your cow fast, throw on some Tchaikovsky, Chopin, or Bach!

FACT 779

Cows eat 100 pounds of grass per day. Need a lawn mower? Consider a cow!

HOLY COW!

MILES MURPHY WAS LOSING SLEEP. He was eating less. Lately people had been saying his face looked a little gray.

"Your face looks a little gray," Holly said when she saw Miles in the hall. "Are you all right?"

Miles Murphy was not all right. For the past two months he'd been anticipating an attack that had never come. He hadn't even been able to enjoy his winter break because he was worried Niles was going to prank him at the mall, or in his house, or when he was hiding from Josh Barkin behind a mailbox. Now that school was back in session, nowhere was safe. They'd been back for three weeks and Niles still hadn't pranked him— probably because of Miles's tireless vigilance. It was a kind of victory, but it felt awful.

Holly walked down the hallway with no hesitation. She rounded corners, waved to kids, smiled at teachers, drummed on lockers as she passed them. She had energy. Charisma.

Miles, meanwhile, kept a step or two behind Holly. He had to. Miles Murphy was at DEFCON 5. Or DEFCON 1. Whichever DEFCON was the most alert, most serious DEFCON. (It was DEFCON 1, a fact Ms. Shandy had mentioned in social studies last Tuesday. But lately Miles hadn't been paying much attention in class, an all-consuming, single-minded readiness being the hallmark of DEFCON 1.)

Holly pointed to a sign on the wall.

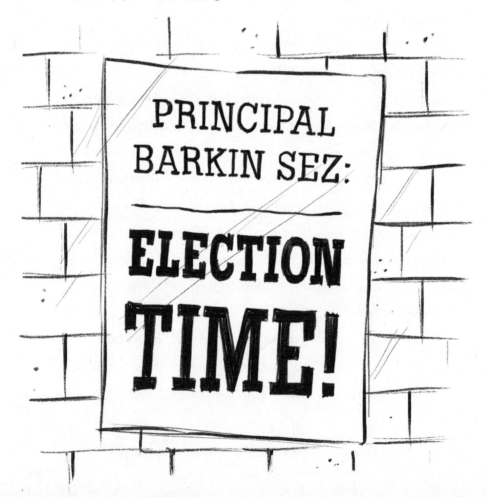

PRINCIPAL BARKIN SEZ:

ELECTION TIME!

The rest of the wall was taken up by a campaign poster: a huge black-and-white photograph of Josh Barkin and his father. The poster was festooned with crepe-paper bunting. Above Josh's head was his slogan.

"I'll bet you he stole those streamers from the art room," Holly said. "And he gets the good real estate, next to the drinking fountain. I had to put mine by the teacher bathroom."

She pointed to another poster down the hall.

A VOTE FOR
HOLLY RASH
IS A
VOTE FOR
HOLLY RASH

She shrugged. "But hey, someone's got to fight the power."

They continued down the hall.

"Good morning, Alice," Holly said to Alice.

"Hey, Scotty," Holly said to a kid presumably named Scotty.

They rounded a corner and there he was.

"Hi, Niles."

"Hi, Holly! Hi, Miles!"

Miles should have looked away. But Niles caught Miles's eye and smiled. Miles's stomach, already sensitive after weeks of a mostly fruit-snack diet, gurgled and churned. Niles's smile was basically an ordinary smile—innocent and sunny, typical of Niles's School Helper mask. But there was something else, something at the corners of Niles's eyes. Confidence. Mischief.

Danger. For weeks this smile had been inducing fear and anger and nausea in Miles. In the middle of class, Niles would turn to Miles and smile. After school, as Miles crossed the parking lot, Niles would wave and smile. At night, Niles's smiling face appeared in Miles's dreams (except in his dreams Niles's head was covered in coarse blond bristles, and he had little red eyes that flashed, and also the dreams took place in the dairy aisle of the supermarket—it was weird). Niles smiled everywhere.

Niles knew Miles hated the smile, and Miles knew Niles knew, and Niles knew Miles knew Niles knew—and somehow all this knowledge was folded back into the smile. The smile was an omen. A portent. The smile meant a prank was coming. Sometimes, late at night, Miles wondered if the smile *was* the prank. But in the mornings, when the sun came through his window, Miles knew he'd never get off that easy.

HOLLY AND MILES STOPPED in front of Miles's new locker, #336. Stuart was entering the combination to the locker below, which was Miles's old locker, #337.

"Hey," said Holly, "when did you get an upper locker?"

"We TRADED," Stuart announced.

"Why would anyone trade—"

Behind Stuart's crouching back, Miles cut Holly off by sawing silently at his neck.

"I KNOW!" Stuart said. "WHY would anyone want an UPPER LOCKER?"

Holly arched an eyebrow. Everyone wanted an upper locker. Miles wanted an upper locker. And, in pretty much the only highlight of the last month or so, he'd tricked Stuart into giving his up.

It was your standard Tom Sawyering: Before lunch one Tuesday, Miles had kneeled in front of his locker and pulled a coin from his pocket.

"Hey, look at that," Miles said. "A quarter."

"WHAT?" said Stuart. "You just FOUND a QUARTER?"

"Yeah. Oh, look at that. It's a bicentennial quarter."

Miles held up the quarter and showed Stuart the drumming man on the back.

"WOW! Aren't those quarters worth even MORE than NOR-MAL QUARTERS?"

"Yeah," said Miles. "About two dollars, I think."

Stuart just looked at the quarter and gasped.

"I find stuff like this on the floor all the time," Miles said. "People are always dropping stuff. It's one reason I love having a lower locker."

"What do you mean ONE reason?"

"Well, you don't have to lift your books into your locker this way. That can lead to injury, you know. Sort of an achy tingling running through your forearm?"

"MY forearm has been ACHING!" Stuart said. "Is that BAD?"

"Could be. Could be tendonitis. Or carpal tunnel."

"Aw MAN!"

"You probably don't have carpal tunnel." Miles pocketed the quarter. "But you never know."

Stuart was looking a little nervous. Time to clinch it.

"Plus a lower locker keeps your lunch fresh and cool. You know—because heat rises."

"I wish I had a LOWER locker."

"Whoa, whoa, Stuart. I'm not going to trade with you."

"PLEASE trade with me!"

"No way. It's not an even trade. I love my lower locker."

"PLEASE."

"Maybe . . ." Miles started. "No."

"WHAT?"

"I was going to say, maybe if you gave me your fruit snacks for a week, but—"

"What about A MONTH?"

And that's how Miles got an upper locker. He looked forward to telling the story to Holly as soon as Stuart left. But Stuart was having trouble with the combination.

"Um, Miles," said Stuart. "What's the last number again?"

"Thirteen."

"Oh YEAH!" Stuart turned the dial to the left. The metal door swung open.

"I don't remember ANY of THIS!" Stuart said.

There was a springing sound and a muffled "*Oof*" from Stuart as a pie flew from his locker and into his face.

This is what Stuart saw in his locker:

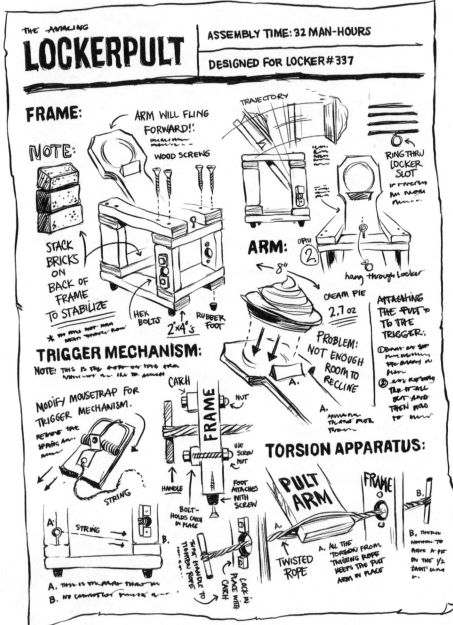

"WHAT the WHAT the WHAT!" Stuart pulled the aluminum pie tin from his face and began to wipe off whipped cream. "That was CRAZY!"

Miles bent down and peered into Stuart's locker. The catapult was impressive. Brilliant, even. The whole prank combined classic styling—a good old pie in the face—with an innovative pie-delivery system. Only Niles Sparks could have dreamed up the contraption in locker #337. But there was one problem: Niles Sparks had gotten the wrong locker.

"Ha, ha!" Miles said. (He actually said, "Ha, ha!") "He didn't know we switched!"

Niles hadn't known about the locker switch. He'd been too busy planning and building and smiling, and he'd missed a crucial detail. Here was a little pranking rule for Niles Sparks: Don't miss crucial details! After a long streak of thwarted pranks, Miles was now the thwarter! He'd thwarted Niles just as Niles had thwarted him! Well, technically he'd benefited from an oversight—it wasn't exactly an active thwarting. But a thwart was a thwart!

Stuart picked off a maraschino cherry stuck above his left eyebrow and popped it in his mouth. "YUM! It's like a SHIRLEY TEMPLE!"

Miles felt a pang of sympathy for Stuart, collateral damage

in the prank war. But then again, he seemed to be enjoying that cherry.

The commotion attracted a crowd, and the crowd attracted Barkin.

"Make way for me, make way for me!" Barkin said. He plowed through the mob and surveyed the situation.

Stuart: Creamed.

Miles: Nearby.

Himself: ON THE CASE.

"Stuart," said Barkin, "you're covered in whipped cream."

"I KNOW!" said Stuart. "There's a PIE-FLINGING machine in my LOCKER!"

"Is there really?" asked Barkin, getting purplish. He examined the inside of Stuart's locker.

"My, my, Barry," the principal muttered to himself. "A catapult."

He pulled a pair of latex gloves from his Principal Pack. "Let's look for clues, shall we?"

Miles already knew what Barkin would find: nothing. Niles may have made one mistake, but he wasn't going to make two.

"Nothing," Barkin said, after some careful poking and prodding. "But the investigation will continue!"

Miles pretended Barkin wasn't staring right at him.

Barkin continued to stare right at him.

The bell rang.

Principal Barkin snapped to purple-faced attention. "Get to class, everybody! That bell means you're late! Don't think I will hesitate to give sixty-two students detentions at once. I would welcome the chance to hold that world record!"

As the crowd dispersed, Miles glimpsed Niles looking on. Niles looked lost. Dismayed. Thwarted.

And for the first time in three weeks, Miles was the one smiling. He grinned at Niles and went to his locker, his upper locker, to grab his math book. Maybe he would have pizza for lunch today. Yes, that sounded pretty good.

He swung open his locker door.

"LOOK at all those CHERRIES!" Stuart said. "It's like your LOCKER is a SHIRLEY TEMPLE FACTORY!"

Miles hoped Barkin wasn't still staring right at him.

He was.

"I didn't do it," said Miles.

"Strike three!" said Principal Barkin.

PRINCIPAL BARKIN WAS RELAXED. He sat back in his chair. His face was not purple or even deep red—it was face colored. Miles took this as a very bad sign.

"I think maybe I was framed," Miles said.

"You were framed," said Barkin. "And who, Miles Murphy, would frame you?"

He couldn't rat. "Lots of people."

"'Lots of people.' Miles Murphy, I don't doubt that lots of people dislike you. But that is because you are a prankster. And now you have just pulled another prank."

"I didn't do it!" said Miles.

"And how do you explain the evidence?"

"A coincidence?"

"Yes, of course! A coincidence! You had a locker full of whipped cream and cherries on the same day Stuart got a face full of whipped cream and cherries. Quite a coincidence! And Stuart's locker, of course, was until Tuesday *your* locker, meaning you had the combination. So really, that's two coincidences!

With all these coincidences, Miles Murphy, I'd suggest you hurry out and buy a lottery ticket, except for one thing: Today is your *unlucky* day."

Miles slouched.

"Another reason I would not suggest you buy a lottery ticket," Barkin continued, "is that it's illegal for a kid to buy a lottery ticket, and so I'd never suggest it. Not that the law ever stopped Miles Murphy! It's also illegal for a kid to drive! And even more illegal for a kid to drive my car! And probably also illegal to park a car at the top of the steps of this school, which I still don't understand how you did!"

"I didn't," Miles said.

Barkin chuckled. "Never in all my years as principal has a car blocked the entrance to this school. Never has a swarm of crickets descended on a classroom full of good students, including my son, Josh, who is a great student. Never have I come across a locker booby-trapped with a pie catapult. And you know what else I'd never seen before this year?"

Barkin extended a surprisingly long index finger. "*You*, Miles Murphy. Now tell me, is that just another coincidence?"

"Yes," Miles said.

"Miles Murphy, do *not* interrupt me! That was a rhetorical question! Don't you even know what a rhetorical question is?"

Miles didn't know whether to answer.

Barkin looked at him expectantly.

"Yes?" Miles said.

"And that was a trick question!" Barkin said. "You were doomed whether you answered it or not. A classic Barkin trap!"

Miles winced.

Outside in the distance, a cow mooed.

"Don't you see, Miles Murphy? You can't win. In fact, you've already lost! The game was over the second you decided to take on a Barkin!"

The principal pushed back his chair and leapt onto his maroon rug.

"The Barkins have been principals at Yawnee Valley for five generations! Right now it's not just me bearing down on you, Miles Murphy. You are feeling the full weight of history on your shoulders. Tango with one Barkin and you tango with all of us!"

Principal Barkin gestured at a wall of portraits in chintzy frames.

"There are only four," Miles said.

"What?"

"There are only four portraits. You said there were five generations of Barkin principals."

"Yes, well. My grandfather's portrait was removed."

For a moment Principal Barkin lost his momentum.

Grandpa Jimmy had been a good man. Always making silver dollars "appear" from behind little Barry's ears. He did the trick every Thanksgiving, the only time Barry's father let Grandpa Jimmy visit. "What's that, some dirt behind your ears?" Grandpa Jimmy would say. Then, reaching forward—*ta-da!*—a silver coin would appear between his grandfather's fingers. And that wasn't even the best part. After a ten-minute speech about the serious real-world importance of behind-the-ear hygiene, emphasizing both cleaning philosophy and technique, Grandpa Jimmy would give Barry the coin, so long as he promised to deposit it in his federally insured Little Saver's College Savings Account. "Compound interest!" Jimmy would say. "That's the real magic trick!"

But Grandpa Jimmy had been soft. He'd canceled school in the Blizzard of '32, besmirching Yawnee Valley's otherwise perfect school-operation record. Principal Barkin remembered the day his father, Former Principal Barkin, then just Principal Barkin, took over this office. "Take it down," Bertrand Barkin had said—those were his First Official Words of Principalship. And so Burt, the janitor, had removed the portrait of James "Jimmy" Barkin from the wall. After school, on the way to his dad's car, Barry saw the painting, its frame cracked, leaning against a green dumpster. He thought about sneaking it home—disobeying his father, stuffing it in the trunk, smuggling it up to his room at night, and hiding it in his closet, behind his blazers.

JAMES "JIMMY" BARKIN – 1930

But he hadn't.

Maybe he should have.

No! Surely Barry Barkin had made the right choice that day! Just as Bertrand had been right to take the portrait down! Because a principal's authority must be absolute! There was no room for weakness!

Principal Barkin's eyes refocused. "Detention. After school. And before school. Every day until you leave this school."

Miles sank.

Chapter 27

MILES HAD NEVER EVEN HEARD of before-school detention. Technically, that wasn't even detention. You had to be at school already to be detained. What would you call it? Prevention. Apprehension. Incarceration.

What was he going to tell his mom?

He walked to the bathroom. Niles Sparks was sitting on a sink.

Miles was too tired to be surprised.

"How did you know I'd come here?"

"First place I'd go if I got all those deten-
tions," Niles said.

Miles went to the next sink and turned on the cold tap. (There was only a cold tap.) He looked in the mirror. He did not look well. He needed sleep. And now he was going to have to wake up early so he could make it to detention.

"Listen, Niles," he said, "I surrender."

"Sorry," said Niles, "I don't accept."

"Niles, I can't do this anymore. I'm not going to have time to prank anymore. You win. Please. Let's end the prank war."

Niles grinned. "Oh, we can end the prank war."

"But you just—"

"I don't accept your surrender." Niles held out his hand. "Truce!"

"But—"

"Oh, come on," Niles said. "Buck up. So I'm ahead right now. You would have gotten me eventually."

Miles wasn't sure that was true.

"It's true!" Niles said. "I keep telling you: You've got real talent. You understand people. And you're quick on your feet. That bacon flyer for Coach O.? Brilliant. The Ten Plagues excuse? I could never have made that up on the spot." He shrugged. "I'm more of a planner."

"Yeah?"

"Yeah! I never wanted this prank war to begin with. Pranksters like us shouldn't be stepping on each other's wingtips."

Miles splashed some water on his face.

"A lot of so-called pranksters," said Niles, "they'd just flush a cherry bomb down that toilet and spend the rest of the school year high-fiving themselves. But we've got ambition. We're visionaries."

Miles had always thought of himself as a bit of a visionary.

"Miles, we need each other."

"We need *each other*? I thought you're always saying how much you can teach me."

"Oh, I can!" Niles said.

Miles rolled his eyes.

"Look, I can teach you things, you can teach me things. Together we'll prank better. We complement each other, blah, blah, blah. Great. Whatever. That's not why we need each other."

The faucet ran.

"Why, then?" Miles asked.

"I need a friend." Niles was matter-of-fact. "And so do you. Pranking is better with a buddy."

Niles held out his hand.

"Truce?"

If Miles shook, well, that was that. They wouldn't just be school buddies. They'd be real buddies. Miles took a good look at the kid perched on the sink. He'd never met anyone like him: a sash-wearing kiss-up with the secret brain of a pranking mastermind. A visionary. A weirdo. Did Miles Murphy really want to be friends with a kid like Niles Sparks?

"Truce."

They shook.

Niles hopped off the sink. "Great. I'm going to go get you off the hook with Barkin."

"Wait, how?"

"Pretty sure it's a violation of chapter thirteen, section two of the disciplinary code to punish you when there's only circumstantial evidence."

"What?"

"You know, stuff that implies you committed a crime but doesn't prove it. I'm going to tell him we should give you some slack and try to catch you red-handed so he can forget about detention and just expel you. He'd love to expel you."

Miles shut off the tap. "OK . . . and so I guess then I just lay low for a while?"

"No way," Niles said, bound for the door. "You and I are going to pull the biggest prank Yawnee Valley's ever seen."

The average person eats forty-eight pints of ice cream a year. Guess who we can thank for all that ice cream? Cows! Have you thanked a cow today?

No two cows have the same set of spots. Their spot patterns are like fingerprints! This is good to know in case a cow robs your bank.

Cows do not rob banks.

CRIKEY!

THE NEXT MORNING there was a rubber chicken in
Miles's locker.

At half past three Miles rang the doorbell
of the big blue house at 47 Buttercream Lane.

Niles answered, sashless.

"You made it."

Miles held up the chicken. "I learned the
telephone cipher in kindergarten."

"You didn't have to bring the chicken."

"Oh yeah. I forgot."

"Come in."

The Sparks residence was tidy and quiet. Niles
led Miles through room after white-carpeted
room. Beige sofas, big TVs, bar stools that swiveled. Blond wood and white leather. "This is the
TV lounge. That's a half bath. Here's the kitchen."

"Are your parents home?" Miles asked.

"Yeah. Dad's in his office, Mom's in her office."

He pointed in opposite directions. "They work from home. Do you want something to drink? We have a bunch of drinks. A soda? I have regular soda and diet soda. Or I have a bunch of natural sodas, which are pretty good, actually. But then I figured you might not drink soda, so I got us a bunch of different juices. And I could make you an Arnold Palmer, which is half lemonade and half iced tea, if you're allowed to drink iced tea."

"I guess I'll just have a glass of water," Miles said.

"Tap water or sparkling water?"

"Tap water's fine."

Niles was clearly disappointed.

"Actually, sparkling sounds good."

"Great!"

Miles and Niles sat on the counter and drank water with bubbles.

"So," said Niles. "I've never had a friend over to my house before. Is this going OK?"

"Sure," said Miles.

"Is this fun? I mean, I thought we should hang out, but I don't know if this is fun."

"It's fun."

Niles took a sip of water. "No, it's not. Come on, I'll show you something cool."

Niles's bedroom looked like it belonged to another house. The carpet had been ripped up to reveal a cherrywood floor that was dark and shiny. There was a deep red rug with golden swirls. A desk and a bed and a big armchair that looked very old. Two large speakers hooked up to a complicated audio system. The tallest globe Miles had ever seen. The rest was books—books piled high in stacks that leaned against the walls and reached almost to the ceiling. If there was an organizing principle to Niles's library, Miles couldn't see it. In one column he saw an atlas, three novels by Louise Fitzhugh, *Accents & Dialects for Stage and Screen*, a joke book, two copies of *Esio Trot*, and volumes on cacti, the Hittites, and thoroughbred racehorses.

"This is amazing," Miles said.

"This isn't the cool part."

Niles opened a door next to his desk. "After you."

"What's in there?" Miles asked.

"Technically it's a walk-in closet, but I don't really need a walk-in closet."

"So what's in there?"

"You'll see."

Miles's scalp tingled. Was this a prank? Wait. Was this all a prank? What if he walked in there and got a bucket of glitter dropped on him, or Niles locked the door behind him and a hundred tarantulas poured out from the walls?

Miles walked into the closet.

Niles closed the door behind them, and everything was dark. He pulled a chain that turned on a lightbulb that hung from the ceiling. The four walls and the ceiling were covered in chalkboard paint, and Miles was surrounded by words and diagrams and maps, all in Niles's tidy handwriting. Some of it was in code. Some was in English. There were a couple of lines in what was maybe French? Directly behind Niles's head was an illegible chart labeled OPERATION: FLOSS ACROSS THE WATER. Written in a corner, behind a milk crate full of dark socks: "A prank that takes place only in the victim's mind." Miles steadied himself against the wall, careful not to smudge anything. It was like walking into a three-dimensional pranking journal.

"Welcome to the prank lab." Niles turned over two crates and sat on the yellow one. Miles took the blue.

"All right," Niles said. "Are you ready to swear the Prankster's Oath?"

"Wait, there really is a Prankster's Oath?"

Niles pulled a yellowed slip of paper out of a penny loafer on the floor. "Of course. Nobody knows who wrote it or when. But it comes from the International Order of Disorder, a loose confederacy of pranksters that flourished a couple of centuries ago. Raise your left hand."

"Shouldn't it be my right hand?"

"That's for normal oaths. You know what 'right' is in French? *Droit*—that means law. But this is the Prankster's Oath—we're outlaws. The Latin word for left is *sinistra*, like 'sinister.' That's us. The mischief makers."

Miles raised his left hand.

"Repeat after me:

On my honor I will do my best

To be good at being bad;

To disrupt, but not destroy;

To embarrass the dour and amuse the merry;

To devote my mind to japes, capers, shenanigans, and monkey business;

To prove the world looks better turned upside down;

For I am a prankster.

So be it."

"So be it," said Miles.

"Perfect," said Niles. "I hereby declare us the sole members of the Yawnee Valley chapter of the International Order of Disorder, hereafter known as the Terrible Two."

"Great," said Miles.

"Hmm," said Niles. "I feel like we need a secret handshake or something."

"Yeah . . ."

They sat on their crates and thought. "I've got it," said Miles. "Hold up two fingers."

Niles did. Miles did too. He touched his fingertips to Niles's.

"High five," said Miles.

"But that's just a high two," said Niles.

"Roman numeral five," said Miles.

Miles grinned.

Niles laughed.

It was official.

And so the Terrible Two got to planning their first prank.

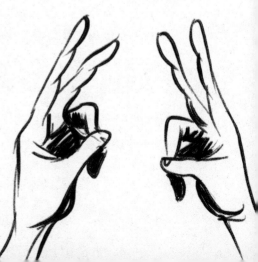

NILES STOOD UP. "What's the best holiday?"

Miles could tell it was a rhetorical question.

Niles continued. "April Fools' Day."

Obviously. Miles nodded.

"On April first, 1698," said Niles, "in England, everyone was invited to the big moat outside the Tower of London to see the lions get washed. That morning, a huge crowd showed up. This was going to be great. Except: There are no lions in the Tower of London. And also: You don't really wash lions."

"No lions, just a bunch of goats," said Miles.

Niles smiled. "Yeah! Exactly! Standing around a stinky ditch. It was the first April Fools' prank. And ever since, April first has been for pranks and hoaxes and practical jokes. As a holiday, there's only one thing wrong with it."

"What's that?" asked Miles.

"We don't get the day off school."

Niles erased a section of one wall with his sleeve. "So. How do we pull a prank so big school gets canceled?"

• • •

Two hours later Miles was sitting in the old armchair and Niles was pacing around his room. There was an empty bowl on the floor and potato chip crumbs and a bunch of crushed soda cans. On one wall of the prank lab was a red square filled with ideas for pranks.

But none of them were good.

Or at least not good enough.

"Well, last time school got canceled, there was a blizzard, right?" said Miles. "Maybe this is stupid, but is there any way we could control the weather?"

Niles thought for a while. "No," he said. "I heard they have machines that can do that in China, but I don't see how we could get our hands on one."

"What if we blocked all the entrances, like you did with Barkin's car?"

"Hmmm," said Niles.

"And by the way, how did you get Barkin's car up there?"

"Let's stay focused," said Niles.

"OK, so we block it with monster trucks."

"Too hard to obtain," Niles said. "Plus everyone could just go underneath them. We could brick up the doors ... but that's too much damage."

"Those crickets weren't bad. I mean, a thousand crickets wouldn't shut down school. But what about a million crickets?"

"That would cost over ten thousand dollars. Plus we'd be repeating ourselves. We need to think bigger."

"Bigger than a million?"

"Bigger than crickets!"

"Cows," Miles said.

"What?"

"Cows."

"But—"

"Cows can walk up stairs but they can't walk down."

Niles stopped pacing. "How do you know that?"

Miles unzipped his backpack and pulled out a crumpled booklet.

1,346 interesting things you may or may not know about cows

by the Yawnee Valley Dairy Council

FOREWORD BY PRINCIPAL BARRY BARKIN

Niles tossed Miles a piece of chalk. "Let's figure this out."

Two weeks, six boxes of cereal, four bags of chips (one original, three sour cream and onion), and a tub of red licorice later, they'd covered one whole wall of the prank lab.

This was going to be great.

Chapter
30

APRIL 1 WAS A MONDAY, fifty-two days away. Most afternoons Miles and Niles went to the library or did research in the prank lab. At lunch they sat together and planned, careful not to seem like they were planning anything. "Looks like you and Niles are getting to be pretty good friends," Holly remarked one day, one eyebrow upraised. "Yep," Miles said, because there was no better cover story than the truth. Holly raised her other eyebrow.

When the snow melted they put on puffy jackets and took tools into the forest by the lake. Together they picked the perfect tree, an old sycamore with a thick, mottled trunk and sturdy white branches spreading out and ending in barren spindles. Miles's mom was so thrilled to hear he was building a tree house with a friend that she chipped in for materials. Niles's parents, who Miles had seen around the house only a few times, financed the rest—Niles had pitched the clubhouse as an engineering project.

They hammered and sawed. It wasn't long before they'd

FEBRUARY 17

FEBRUARY 24

MARCH 1

MARCH 31

built a platform, and then a roof. Even though it was cold, they brought books to the tree and read in the gray light of winter. It got warm enough to camp out. They brought Niles's red tent to the tree and set it up on the platform. Miles was in charge of setting it up and taking it down. Niles was in charge of marshmallows. In March their tree grew great green leaves, and the clubhouse got walls and a window.

"It's perfect," Niles said, when the tree house was done.

Miles painted SECRET HQ above the doorway, and they carved initials next to the window. They made their final April Fools' preparations nineteen feet above the ground, and then there was nothing left to do but prank.

Chapter 31

OFFICIALLY THE PRANK BEGAN on March 23, when Miles Murphy deposited a letter in the mailbox on his corner, but the real action didn't get under way till midnight on April 1. Miles watched the red numbers on his alarm clock change from 11:59 to 12:00. The last verse of "These Boots Are Made for Walking" started playing softly, but Miles was already awake. He hadn't gone to sleep. About two hours ago he'd given

up on the book that he was too distracted to read, and he'd been staring at the radio since then, going over the plan, waiting for the tiny click his alarm clock made before the music came on. Miles grabbed his backpack. He'd hoped he'd be too tired to be anxious, or too wired to be anxious, but he was anxious. And tired. And wired.

"Happy April Fools' Day," he said. Time to go.

Miles had sort of wanted to make a rope with his bedsheets, but his mom was a deep sleeper. The smartest thing was to sneak downstairs and out his front door. Stars spilled overhead, and the night's cold air made his lungs ache. The only sound was the faint buzz of a streetlight on the fritz. Miles Murphy realized he'd never been out this late on his own before. It was exhilarating. He pulled up the hood of his sweatshirt and took off down the street.

When Miles saw headlights he froze. Bent over, he pretended to tie his shoe. Act natural. He was ready for the car to slow down, ask him what he was doing, a kid out at night, and on April Fools' Day too. But the car drove right by. After that Miles didn't stop for anything.

On Spring Street a raccoon crawled out of a storm drain and stared at him like he knew exactly what Miles was up to and like he was in on it. They were two of a kind, Miles and this

raccoon! Masked bandits, denizens of the night! Miles saluted the raccoon as he ran past. The raccoon went back down the drain.

Soon there were no more street-lights, just darkness, but Miles knew where he was going. Paved road gave way to dirt road gave way to no road. Miles hopped a fence. The grass grew tall here and the dew soaked his jeans to midcalf. When he made it to the meadow, where the trees grew thick, it was safe to use the flashlight, just for a second. He caught his breath, got his bearings, flicked the switch to off. He had to move slower now, stepping carefully over roots and easing down gullies. Almost there.

At the rendezvous point, he pressed a button on his watch and the face lit up. Eleven minutes early. He leaned against a maple tree and waited.

A steady creaking came at 1:00. It grew louder and stopped nearby. Miles flashed his light three times. Three blinks answered. Niles pulled up on a bike, pulling Miles's wagon behind him. The wagon held a small bale of hay.

"This thing feels heavier tonight," Niles said. He hopped off his bike. He was wearing black jeans, a black sweatshirt, and a tall black Stetson.

"What's with the hat?" Miles asked.

"It felt appropriate."

Part of Miles wanted to make fun of the hat. The other part wanted a hat.

"Let's do this," said Miles.

Chapter 32

NILES RUBBED HIS HANDS TOGETHER. He

blew into his fists. It was the first time Miles had ever seen Niles nervous.

Niles raised his hands to his mouth. His voice was startling in the blackness.

"Hey, boss! Heyyyyyyyyyyyy, boss! Hup, hup!"

Nothing happened.

That wasn't good.

"Um, it's fine," Niles said. "Different farmers use different calls."

"OK," Miles said.

Niles cried out again: "Sue, boss! Suuuuuuuuuuue, boss!"

Silence.

A sheepish shrug from Niles.

Miles chewed on his thumb. This part had not been his responsibility. Maybe it should have been.

"I've got some more." Niles cleared his throat. "Come, boss! Cooooooooooooome, boss!"

Somewhere nearby, a cow mooed.

And so did another cow.

And another.

The night was full of the moos of cows. The moos were nearby, and they were getting closer.

"Coooooooooooome, boss!" said Niles.

"Moo," said the cows.

"Ha, ha!" said Miles, except he didn't say it. He was actually laughing.

A big cow-shaped shadow came over the hill, mooing and ringing.

"Hey, Bossie!" said Niles. "She's got a bell around her neck—that's the lead cow!"

Now the cows came from all over, up from the gully, out from the trees. The meadow filled with one of Bob Barkin's dairy herds, perhaps wondering why this morning's milking was starting so early, but probably not. After all, they were cows.

Bossie was getting close now, and some of the cows were beginning to fall in behind her. Niles clapped his hands. "OK, let's go!" Niles hopped on the bike. "Come, boss!" he shouted. He reached back and threw a handful of hay in the direction of the approaching herd. Bossie scooped it up without stopping and kept moving toward Niles. Standing up on the pedals, Niles Sparks started to ride. Bossie followed the hay, and the cows followed Bossie.

Miles had a job to do.

Chapter 33

IN ALMOST TWO MONTHS of reading about moving cows, Miles Murphy's favorite bit was a passage from J. M. Iverson's *Herding with Dignity*:

"Every creature on earth is either predator or prey. A cow is a prey animal. Cows think like prey. They react like prey. If you want to move cows, you've got to move like a predator."

Miles eyed the herd. They were ambling around in a clump, calves and cows both, sort of following Niles's bike as he pedaled through the pasture. But some were moving in the wrong direction. Some just stood there. More than a few were munching on grass.

Miles ducked into a low crouch. "You're a coyote," Miles thought. He sprang forward.

Tense and graceful, Miles moved across the grass. As he approached the rear of the herd, the stragglers raised their heads. Their ears perked up. They mooed. They turned toward Miles and stared him down. And then they started moving.

Miles moved toward the cows. They moved away.

And now the whole clump was going, following Niles on the bike down a knoll, with Miles bringing up the rear. Miles was zigzagging, back and forth, to the outer edges of the herd. Side to side, side to side, like a coyote, the cows

getting jumpy. They bucked, they snorted, they farted and tossed their tails. Miles felt their resistance and kept sweeping from side to side, pressing the animals forward. You're a coyote. You're a coyote.

As they crested a low rise, a single cow spooked and trotted off from the herd. Miles wanted to chase, but he swallowed his instinct and let her go. Ten seconds later she stopped, swiveled her head nervously, and rejoined the procession. It was just like Iverson had said in chapter one, paragraph one—cows liked to stay together.

After a quarter mile, the herd had thinned out into a line, walking two or three abreast. They were really mooing now. The adults were in the front, the calves, jumpy and gawky, behind. Bringing up the rear were what must have been the oldest cows, grumpy, reluctant, moaning. And then Miles zigging, zagging, a coyote.

Miles did a rough count. They were riding herd on more than a hundred head of cattle. He was pretty sure he was using all those terms the right way. Forward, forward, into the night. He could feel the momentum.

"Gate!" Niles called out from his bike. "Gate!"

Miles dropped back and let the line get ahead. Then he peeled off far to the left and sprinted past calves, past cows, past Niles and the hay. He ran through white puffs of his own breath, throwing himself against the metal fence. The latch was a cold shock against his bare hands, and Miles used his whole body to swing the gate open. There was the bang of the gate and the clang of Bossie's cowbell and the squeaking of Niles's bike. Miles ran alongside the fence for a while, picked a spot to climb over, and dropped down to the ground. Then he was up again and running as fast as he could.

Niles was getting close to the gate, the herd right behind him. Miles had to make it back to the rear of the line. He took his position in time to see Niles coast through the gate, tossing some hay over his shoulder. "Come, boss! Cooooooooommmmme, boss!" Bossie was through, then the next two cows, then more. Miles pressed forward, willing the cows to move, to walk on. Get through the gate. Get through the gate. He was relentless, alert to the motion of the herd and the movements of individual cows. Miles breathed in the heat from their bodies. Their smell, rich and sweet, was in his nose and in his throat.

And soon all the cows were through the gate and so was Miles. He stopped to take a breath. Up ahead, his friend was riding a bike in the light of a rising moon, and Miles was here, breathing, and there was a line of one hundred cows between them. It was after midnight and nobody—not Miles, not Niles, not the cows—was where they were supposed to be, and that felt right. Miles dropped to a crouch and sank his fingers into the damp earth. In the soil, beetles shuddered, worms tunneled, grass strived upward. Miles could feel it all in his fingertips.

Niles rode on and the cows followed, away from the gate, away from the fence, away from Bob Barkin's farm.

Niles pumped a fist into the air. Miles howled at the sky.

A **LINE OF COWS** five hundred feet long proceeded two by two down Chapman Drive, one of the quietest streets in the sleepy town of Yawnee Valley. Niles and Miles had plotted their route carefully. It was 3:13 A.M. and nobody was out.

Niles rang the bell on his bike twice. Intersection.

Then Miles was sprinting again, up on the lawns, hopping hedges, maybe trampling a couple of early-blooming flower beds. He arrived at the corner of Chapman and Trellis well before Niles, who was weaving slowly to give Miles plenty of time to unshoulder his backpack and take out Niles's quick-pitch tent. He tossed it into the air with a flick of the wrist, and the tent *sproinged* as it unfolded at the peak of its arc. It landed and bounced. Miles positioned the tent on one side of the intersection, blocking off Trellis Drive in one direction. At least that was the idea. The tent looked puny now in the middle of the road, and Miles hoped it was enough to discourage the cows from bolting off down the wrong street. It would have to be. Miles took his position on the other side of Trellis. Niles cruised by wearing a madman's grin.

And then the cows.

They gave him placid looks, wild looks, accusing looks. The cows were close enough for Miles to touch. So he did. The cow flinched when Miles reached out and brushed his hand against her flank. Her hair was coarse and damp and warm. Miles put his hand to his nose. He smelled like an animal. It was the first time Miles had touched a cow.

The old cows dragged past and the intersection was clear. It was time to fold up the tent. This was supposed to be simple, but Miles had never gotten the hang of it. The idea was the same as the collapsible silver sunshade Miles's mom had in her car, but Miles had never been able to figure that out either. After wrestling the tent for about a minute, Miles had gotten it down to a poky misshapen lump small enough to fit back in the backpack. Miles took off down the road and caught up with the herd just in time to hear Niles ring his bell twice again.

There were six more intersections on their path that night, and by the fourth Miles was running down the street hugging the pitched tent in front of himself. He fumbled. He tripped. But they made it without losing a single cow. And by 3:56 they were making their way down Sunnyslope Road—the homestretch.

Five urgent rings from Niles's bell. They had company. At the head of the line Niles was waving to a figure standing in the middle of a house's front lawn. As Miles got closer he saw it was a man, an old man, wearing nothing but his boxer shorts. The man stood agog, watching the cows parade by his house. "If anyone sees us, and they probably won't," Niles had said back in the prank lab, "just play it by ear. You're good in the moment." Miles tried to take a nervous gulp, but his throat was too tight. By the time he'd made it up to the man's mailbox, he still hadn't figured out what to say.

It turned out the man wasn't wearing just boxers—he also had a terry-cloth sweatband around his head. His white hair was uncombed and shone in the moonlight.

They were so close. If this all fell apart now—

"What are you doing in the middle of town with all these cows?" asked the man.

"What are you doing out in your underwear at four in the morning?" Miles replied.

"Fair enough," said the man.

And that was that.

Eight minutes later Niles led the cows up the driveway to Yawnee Valley Science and Letters Academy. He leapt off his bike and dragged the wagon up the front steps, spilling hay as he went. The key ring Niles pulled out was so big Miles could see it from the back of the herd. Niles fiddled with the lock and slipped inside. In less than five seconds the front hall glowed yellow. Niles threw the doors open. Niles pitched some more hay onto the threshold. "Coooooooooome, boss," he said, then disappeared inside, dragging the wagon behind him.

Bossie sniffed the steps. She snorted and moaned. Then she took the steps in two clumsy hops. Her head was inside. Then her withers. Then her rump and her tail. And then the next cow.

Miles pushed forward against the herd's misgivings, exerting steady pressure from behind. The cows disliked Miles more than they disliked stairs. And they loved moving together. It took only six minutes to get 107 cows through the front door of Yawnee Valley Science and Letters Academy.

When the last rump was through, Miles shut the door.

He waited outside.

Niles flipped off the lights and slammed the front door shut. "Happy April Fools' Day," he said.

Miles and Niles collapsed on their backs on the school's wet grass.

Miles held two fingers right up to the sky. "High five."

Niles held up his two. "High five."

Then they laughed.

And they laughed.

Chapter 35

THE BARKINS' PHONE RANG at 4:03 A.M.

Principal Barkin picked it up and said, "Mmmmpfffff."

"BARRY, THIS IS YOUR FATHER, FORMER PRINCIPAL BARKIN. AM I WAKING YOU UP?"

"No," said Principal Barkin.

"DON'T LIE TO ME! I CAN HEAR THE SLEEP IN YOUR VOICE."

"Is something wrong?" asked Principal Barkin.

"DO YOU KNOW WHAT TODAY IS?"

"It's—"

"IT'S APRIL FIRST, ALSO KNOWN AS APRIL FOOLS' DAY, AND YOU ARE SLEEPING! LIKE A FOOL! YOU SHOULD BE UP WRITING YOUR APRIL FOOLS' POWER SPEECH."

"I wrote it last night," said Principal Barkin.

"THEN YOU SHOULD BE UP PRACTICING!"

"OK."

"PLANNING YOUR PAUSES!"

"OK."

"PUTTING POWER INTO YOUR VOICE!"

"OK."

"ENSURING THAT EVERY STUDENT KNOWS THERE WILL BE ZERO TOLERANCE FOR APRIL FOOLS' PRANKS."

"You know, Dad," said Principal Barkin, "some people might say calling a person at four in the morning is an April Fools' prank."

"HOW DARE YOU! THIS IS NOT A PRANK. I AM NOT PRANKING YOU RIGHT NOW. I HAVE NEVER PRANKED IN MY LIFE."

"That was a joke, Dad."

"A JOKE? OR A PRANK? THERE'S A FINE LINE BE-TWEEN 'JOKE' AND 'PRANK,' BARRY, AND YOU'RE STEPPING RIGHT UP TO THAT LINE WHEN YOU ACCUSE YOUR FATHER OF PRANKING. A PRANK-ING PRINCIPAL! JUST LIKE YOUR GRANDPA JIMMY. YOU KNOW, HE ONCE—"

"I better go practice this speech, Dad."

"THEN GO!"

"Bye."

"GIVE JOSH AND SHARON MY LOVE."

Barry Barkin sat on the edge of his bed in the dark.

"That was my father," he told his wife. "He sends his love."

"Mmmmpfffff," said Mrs. Barkin.

Principal Barkin couldn't get back to sleep. When he closed his eyes he saw Miles Murphy's face. That little prankster was probably planning something. Principal Barkin decided that his father was right. His father was always right.

He turned on his bedside lamp.

At 6:03, Principal Barkin, showered, shaved, and full of oatmeal on toast, pulled into his parking spot behind the school. He activated his new car alarm and walked up the steps to the rear entrance of Yawnee Valley Science and Letters Academy.

Barkin sniffed. It smelled like cows this morning. Must be a strong wind blowing in from the farmland.

Barkin entered the school. In the dark, on the way to the light switch, he bumped into something large and hairy. "I don't remember any of this," he mumbled.

Barkin flipped on the lights.

It was a cow.

Barkin almost laughed.

"April Fools,'" he said to the cow.

Principal Barkin had a list of suspects that was exactly one kid long. Apparently this was Miles Murphy's idea of an April Fools' joke. Too bad Miles didn't know his principal liked to get to school early. Principal Barkin had plenty of time to lead this cow out the back door and down those—

Principal Barkin put his hand on his Principal Pack.

Fact 586.

That cow couldn't get down stairs.

Fine! This was fine. He had plenty of time to squash this April Fools' joke. The earliest students wouldn't be arriving for almost an hour. That was plenty of time to hide this cow in his office.

"This way, cow," Principal Barkin said to the cow.

The cow didn't say anything.

Soon Principal Barkin was behind the cow, pushing. Then he was in front of the cow, pulling. The cow didn't move.

"Move, cow!" said Principal Barkin, now behind the cow again.

That's when a second cow, curious about the commotion, rounded the corner.

"Two cows!" said Principal Barkin. This prank was more elaborate than he'd thought. Barkin wasn't sure he could fit two cows in his office. Maybe he could stash one in the faculty bathroom.

A third cow ambled over.

Barry Barkin began to get a terrible feeling.

He tiptoed to the corner and peered around.

"No," said Principal Barkin. "No, no, no, no, no, no, no, no."

He ran down the halls. He saw more cows.

"No no no no no no no no no no no no no no no no no no no no no no no!"

Cows in classrooms.

"NO NO NO NO NO NO NO NO NO NO NO NO NO NO NO NO NO NO NO!"

This was bad. This was very bad. Barkin needed an idea. Some way to salvage the school day. He needed a place to think.

A place away from all these cows. He ran up the stairs, pushed through more cows, and opened the door to the supply closet. His sanctuary. His fortress.

He turned on the light.

"No."

A cow was chewing on a mop. It was the masterstroke.

AT 7:45, MILES AND NILES crossed the parking lot and joined a throng of students amassed on the lawn. Principal Barkin had a bullhorn. He was barring the entrance. Later, students would agree that Barkin's face had never been so purple. It looked like his neck held up a screaming bilberry.

"I REPEAT, FORM AN ORDERLY CLUMP."

"What's going on?" asked Holly.

"Yeah!" said that guy Scotty. "What's going on?"

"WHAT'S GOING ON IS THAT YOU CAN'T COME INTO SCHOOL RIGHT NOW BECAUSE . . . BECAUSE IT IS ON FIRE."

Panic. Screaming.

"*WAS* ON FIRE! *WAS* ON FIRE! A SMALL FIRE THAT IS OUT. REMAIN ON THE PREMISES! EVERYTHING IS SAFE!"

"If it's safe, why can't we go inside?" asked Ms. Shandy.

"UMM . . . BECAUSE THERE IS A FLOOD. LUCKILY THE FLOOD PUT OUT THE SMALL FIRE, BUT NOW THERE IS A LOT OF WATER. REMAIN IN A CLUMP. THE SCHOOL DAY WILL COMMENCE SHORTLY."

"It SMELLS like a COW!" said Stuart.

"WHAT? NO. THAT IS JUST THE SMELL OF BURNED THINGS THAT ARE NOW WET. WHEN SOMETHING IS ON FIRE AND THEN GETS FLOODED IT SOMETIMES MAKES A COW SMELL."

Somewhere in the art room, a cow mooed.

"That *sounded* like a cow," said Holly.

"RIDICULOUS. WHAT IS MORE LIKELY, HOLLY? THAT WE HAD A FIRE AND A FLOOD, OR THAT THERE ARE COWS IN SCHOOL?"

"I guess the fire and flood?"

"EXACTLY, HOLLY. EXACTLY."

"There's a COW in the ART ROOM!" Stuart said. He had his hands cupped against the window and was peering inside.

"STUART, STEP AWAY FROM THE BUILDING."

"There are SIX cows in the art room!"

Chaos. Laughter.

"STUDENTS! ALL STUDENTS! PRINCIPAL BAR-
KIN SEZ: STEP AWAY FROM THE BUILDING. STOP
LOOKING THROUGH THE WINDOWS."

"There are COWS EVERYWHERE!" Stuart said.

Bossie came up to the window behind Barkin.

"Well, isn't this something," said Holly.

"ANOTHER cow!" said Stuart. "This is like COW CITY!"

Bossie's breath left a thick coating of cud on the glass.

"THERE IS NOTHING REMARKABLE HAPPEN-
ING!" shouted Barkin.

"I think the cat's out of the bag, Barry," said Ms. Shandy.

"LEAVE! GO HOME! STOP LOOKING! GO AWAY!"
Principal Barkin said. "SCHOOL IS CANCELED!"

Mayhem. Cheering.

MILES WENT OVER TO NILES'S house for a cele-
bratory breakfast: cereal and toast with three kinds of
jam and scrambled eggs with onions, all washed down with a
big glass of milk. It was delicious.

But the prank wasn't quite finished.

At about 10:30, Miles and Niles returned to school.

They found Barkin behind the school, where he'd gone with
his son after the students had left that morning. For a while,
Josh had tried to push a cow out the rear exit.

"It won't go down the steps, Dad!"

"Of course she won't!" Principal Barkin had said. "Haven't
you even read the booklet? You're not helping. Go home."

He'd called his wife to pick Josh up and spent the next couple
of hours sitting.

"Niles, am I glad to see you," said Principal Barkin when he
saw the pair approach. "Miles, I am not glad to see you. Unless
you're here because Niles can prove that you put these cows in
the school, and he is here to turn you in."

"I didn't do it," Miles said.

"That's what you always say," said Principal Barkin. "You should put that on a T-shirt. And then I will wear a T-shirt that says YES YOU DID."

"Principal Barkin," said Niles, "Miles couldn't have done it."

Barkin stared at his School Helper. "Why not?"

"Because Miles spent the night at my house."

"On a school night?"

"We were studying for Ms. Shandy's test," Niles said.

"Test." Principal Barkin exhaled faintly. "School canceled on a test day."

"And election day!" Niles said. "We were supposed to vote for class president."

Principal Barkin's gaze went fuzzy.

"It looks like the cows are still here," said Miles.

"Of course they are," said Principal Barkin. "They can't go down steps. Doesn't anyone read the booklet?"

"Hey, maybe you should call your brother!" said Niles. "Isn't he a farmer?"

"I can't. They're all branded 'B.' They're his cows."

"Oh!" said Niles. "So then . . . shouldn't you tell him?"

"No, no, no . . . Bob has a big mouth and—you boys wouldn't

understand. Thanks for coming, but I'm afraid you can't be of much help, Niles. And Miles, you can be of even less help."

"Actually," said Niles, "we think we figured out who did this. We think we know who did all the pranks."

Barkin snapped upright. "You do?"

"Yeah," said Miles. "We think . . . well, we think . . ."

"We think it was Josh," said Niles.

"Josh who?" said Principal Barkin.

"Josh Barkin," said Miles.

"Josh, my son, Barkin?" said Principal Barkin.

"Yes," said Niles.

"THAT'S INSANE!" said Principal Barkin.

"Is it?" said Niles. "Think about it. He would have access to your car keys. And the keys to the school. And even the locker combinations! Maybe Josh is the one who framed Miles with that pie catapult. I mean, we know Josh doesn't like Miles."

"Well, nobody likes Miles. He's a prankster."

"But what if he's not?"

Barkin hesitated.

"But no! Josh couldn't have! He was at Cody Burr-Tyler's Nature Scout Outdoor Jamboree last night!"

"On a school night?" Niles said.

"Well, you boys understand . . ." said Barkin. "It was *Cody Burr-Tyler* . . ."

Miles smiled.

"Principal Barkin," Miles said, "Cody Burr-Tyler doesn't even exist."

"NOW *THAT* IS INSANE."

"That *is* insane," said Niles. "We went to his birthday party! I bought that guy a present!"

"I met some kids from St. Perpetua the other week," Miles said. "They'd never heard of him."

"But then who'd I give a present to?" Niles asked. "Who'd we all give presents to? Who was wearing that football helmet? Unless . . ."

"I mean, Josh was basically the only kid who was not at the party . . ."

"No, no, no, no. I have the invitation to the jamboree right here. See. From Cody Burr-Tyler."

Barkin pulled out a card from his Principal Pack.

Niles took a look. "Red ink." He drew in a slow, tragic breath and shook his head. "I hate to say it, but this could be a forgery, Principal Barkin. Josh was the only student to fill out my midyear wellness survey in red . . ."

Dear Josh Barkin,
This is your good friend Cody Burr-Tyler, inviting you to join me at my annual Nature Scout Outdoor Jamboree, a campout on the night of MARCH 31. For one hundred years this event has been held on the last day before April (which unfortunately falls on a school night this year) as an opportunity to renew our virtue and respect each spring. I hope you can make it. I promise we'll get plenty of sleep and my dad will get you to school on time!

Respectfully,

Cody Burr-Tyler

For once, Barkin didn't go purple. He went pale. "Excuse me, boys. I have to make a phone call."

Earlier that week, Josh Barkin had received an invitation from Cody Burr-Tyler. But it hadn't been to a jamboree. And it hadn't been written in red ink. It was written with a blue Bic Velocity 1.6-millimeter ballpoint pen and mailed by Miles Murphy on March 23. Here is what it said.

Dear Josh Barkin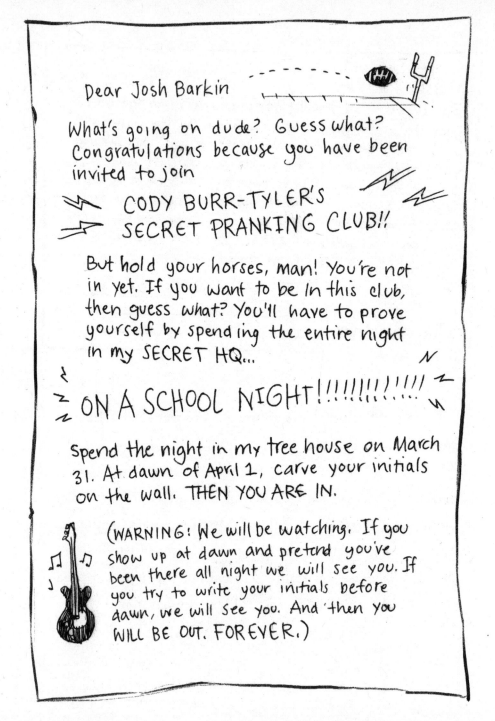

What's going on dude? Guess what? Congratulations because you have been invited to join

CODY BURR-TYLER'S SECRET PRANKING CLUB!!

But hold your horses, man! You're not in yet. If you want to be In this club, then guess what? You'll have to prove yourself by spending the entire night in my SECRET HQ...

ON A SCHOOL NIGHT!!!!!!!!!!!!!!

Spend the night in my tree house on March 31. At dawn of April 1, carve your initials on the wall. THEN YOU ARE IN.

(WARNING: We will be watching. If you show up at dawn and pretend you've been there all night we will see you. If you try to write your initials before dawn, we will see you. And then you WILL BE OUT. FOREVER.)

How are you gonna pull this off?
That's your problem! Make something
up. Tell your folks you're hanging
out at my Nature Scout Jamboree or...
wait... why am I giving you ideas?
YOU THINK OF SOMETHING.

DESTROY THIS MESSAGE AS
SOON AS YOU READ IT. EAT IT
OR SOMETHING, OR ELSE.

— CODY

It took a brief principal-to-principal call for Barkin to verify that Miles and Niles were right: Nobody named Cody Burr-Tyler was enrolled at St. Perpetua. But at home Josh Barkin swore Cody was real. "OK, so I wasn't at his Jamboree. But I couldn't have moved Uncle Bob's cows. I was spending the night at Cody Burr-Tyler's Secret HQ. I even carved my initials in the wall! With the date! I'll show you."

And so Principal Barkin followed Josh into the forest. But while the perfect tree house takes hammers, saws, and six weeks to build, it only takes a sledgehammer, a delicious breakfast, and a couple of hours to dismantle completely.

"But . . ." Josh Barkin stood at the base of a sycamore, looking up at branches that held only the beginnings of buds that would soon bloom bright red.

"I want you to walk out of this forest, back to our house, and up to your room," said Principal Barkin. "You are grounded. And, although it pains me to say it, you are officially on probation at Yawnee Valley Science and Letters Academy."

APRIL 1

"But you can't put me on probation. That would mean—"

"Yes, that would mean you are ineligible for student council. When we reschedule school elections, Holly Rash will be running unopposed."

Josh turned his back and muttered, "Nimbus."

But Principal Barkin wasn't finished. "And, Josh," he said. "I certainly *can* put you on probation. I can do anything. I am a principal."

Principal Barkin straightened his red tie. He'd had a pretty bad day, but that was a pretty good power speech.

THE BEST WAY TO GET COWS down a short flight of stairs is to build a ramp by covering the steps with a few sheets of thick plywood. (It's also the best way to get a car up a flight of stairs.) By the time Bob Barkin showed up in his truck and built just such a ramp, Miles Murphy was already asleep.

It was the earliest Miles had ever gone to bed, including sick days. After Miles left school for the second time that day, he'd gone straight home and found his wagon waiting on the front porch. There was a present inside, wrapped in green with a yellow ribbon. He opened it up in his room. In a shoe box, wrapped in tissue paper, was a sash that said SCHOOL HELPER HELPER. He tried it on. Maybe it was just the exhaustion, but he liked how it looked.

Miles Murphy brushed his teeth and got into bed. He put his pranking journal underneath his pillow. The sun streamed through his window, but he didn't pull the shade.

Miles Murphy was a cowboy. A cattle rustler. A pranking legend. And nobody knew it. Except himself. And Niles

Sparks. And that was good, and his bed was warm, and it wasn't long before Miles was sleeping the best sleep he'd slept since he moved to Yawnee Valley.

Somewhere in the distance, a cow mooed.

OTHER BOOKS BY
MAC BARNETT *and* **JORY JOHN**

The Terrible Two Get Worse
The Terrible Two Go Wild
The Terrible Two's Last Laugh

ABOUT *the* AUTHORS

MAC BARNETT is a *New York Times* bestselling author of many books for children, including *Extra Yarn*, illustrated by Jon Klassen, which won a 2013 Caldecott Honor and the 2012 *Boston Globe–Horn Book* Award for Excellence in Picture Books; *Sam & Dave Dig a Hole*, also illustrated by Jon Klassen; and *Battle Bunny*, written with Jon Scieszka and illustrated by Matthew Myers. He also writes the Brixton Brothers series of mystery novels.

JORY JOHN is a *New York Times* bestselling author of books for both children and adults. He is a two-time E.B. White Read-Aloud Honor recipient. Jory's work includes the picture books *Giraffe Problems* and *Penguin Problems*, both illustrated by Lane Smith, the Goodnight Already! series, illustrated by Benji Davies, *The Bad Seed* and *The Good Egg*, both illustrated by Pete Oswald, and the award-winning *Quit Calling Me a Monster!*, illustrated by Bob Shea. He also co-authored numerous humor books, including the internationally bestselling *All My Friends Are Dead*. Jory spent six years as programs director at 826 Valencia, a nonprofit educational center in San Francisco. He resides in Oregon.

KEVIN CORNELL is the illustrator of many children's books, including *Count the Monkeys* and *Mustache!*, both by Mac Barnett.

FOR TAYLOR
—MB

THIS BOOK IS DEDICATED TO ALYSSA; MY MOM, DEBORAH; AND STEVEN MALK,
WHO BELIEVED IN THIS PROJECT FROM THE START. I WILL CONTINUE THANKING
THE THREE OF YOU UNTIL THE COWS COME HOME, WHICH MIGHT TAKE A WHILE.
—JJ

Library of Congress Cataloging-in-Publication Data
Barnett, Mac.
The terrible two / by Mac Barnett & Jory John ; illustrated by Kevin Cornell.
pages cm — (The terrible two)
Summary: When master prankster Miles Murphy moves to sleepy Yawnee Valley, he challenges the local mystery prankster in an epic battle of tricks, but soon the two join forces to pull off the biggest prank ever seen.
ISBN 978-1-4197-1491-7 (hardcover) — ISBN 978-1-61312-763-6 (ebook)
[1. Practical jokes—Fiction. 2. Tricks—Fiction. 3. Schools—Fiction. 4. Moving, Household—Fiction. 5. Humorous stories.] I. Barnett, Mac. II. Cornell, Kevin, illustrator. III. Title.
PZ7.J62168Ter 2015
[Fic]—dc23
2014027503

ISBN 978-1-4197-2737-5 (paperback)
Text copyright © 2015 Mac Barnett, Jory John
Illustrations copyright © 2015, 2016 Kevin Cornell
Chapter from *The Terrible Two Get Worse* text copyright © 2016 Mac Barnett, Jory John
Book design by Chad W. Beckerman

Printed and bound in U.S.A.
10 9

ABRAMS The Art of Books
195 Broadway, New York, NY 10007
abramsbooks.com

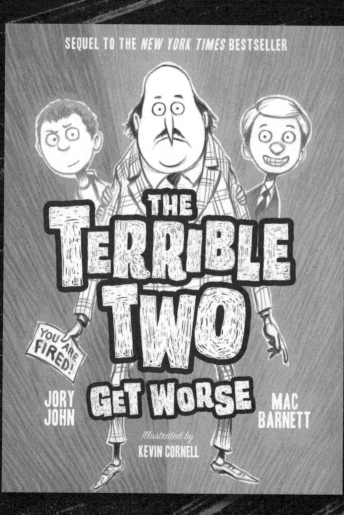

WELCOME BACK TO YAWNEE VALLEY, its

green hills and cows, cows, cows. The grass grows, the hills roll, the cows moo. Who cares?

Well, these two.

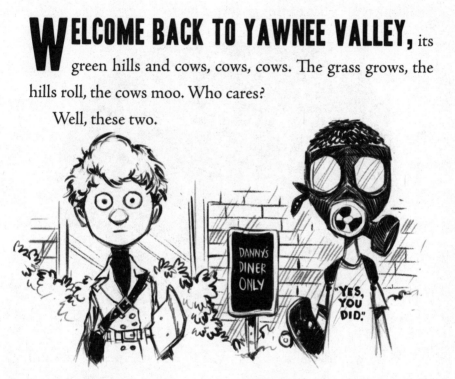

This is Miles Murphy and Niles Sparks, the only members of a two-person secret club known to themselves and only themselves as the Terrible Two. (Miles is the one in a gas mask.)

The Terrible Two was a particular kind of secret club. The Terrible Two was a pranking club. And on this day, a Sunday, Miles and Niles were about to pull their latest prank.

On the day before this day, a Saturday, Miles and Niles had drawn up a list of things they'd need:

"Why would we need gas masks?" asked Niles. Miles and Niles were in their prank lab, a walk-in closet off Niles's bedroom whose four walls and ceiling had been covered in chalkboard paint so the Terrible Two could plot out their pranks.

Notice the maps. Notice the diagrams. Notice the crate full of black socks stuck in the corner.

The socks aren't important. But behind the socks was something very important. Behind the socks were fifty-eight words Miles and Niles lived by.

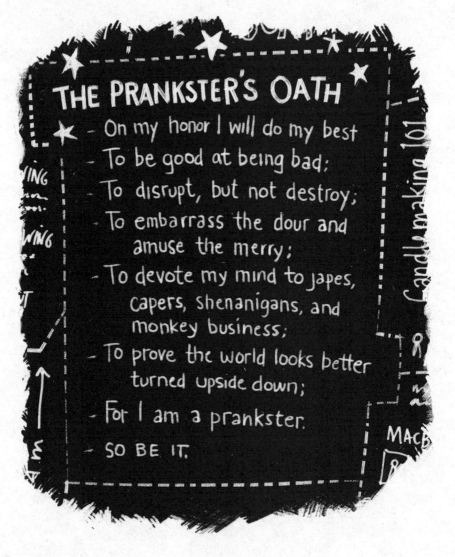

THE PRANKSTER'S OATH
- On my honor I will do my best
- To be good at being bad;
- To disrupt, but not destroy;
- To embarrass the dour and amuse the merry;
- To devote my mind to japes, capers, shenanigans, and monkey business;
- To prove the world looks better turned upside down;
- For I am a prankster.
- SO BE IT.

(If you're reading this book somewhere quiet, someplace alone where no one will hear you, feel free to raise your left hand—the prankster's hand—and say those words yourself.)

"And that's why we need gas masks," said Miles, who'd been talking this whole time.

"I don't think gas masks work like you think they work," said Niles.

"I think they work exactly like I think they work," said Miles.

"Well, yeah," said Niles. "That's the definition of thinking."

"*I'm* bringing a gas mask," said Miles. "And I'll bring one for you too. I'll bet you want it tomorrow."

Which is how we got here.

"Are you sure you don't want one?" Miles asked.

"Yes."

Niles pulled a clothespin out of his pocket and used it to clip his nostrils shut. He winced a little, because it hurt.

"The gas mask would be way more comfortable," said Miles.

"OK," said Niles.

"Plus it looks really cool."

Niles took a good look at Miles.

"Maybe," he said.

Miles and Niles laid the skateboards on the pavement. (Both skateboards belonged to Miles. This morning he'd ridden one over to the parking lot behind Danny's Diner. Niles had carried the other one. He didn't have very good balance.)

They put on their rubber gloves.

They pulled out their paintbrushes.

Then Miles reached into his backpack and removed the most important thing they needed for this morning's prank, something too important to include on their list, lest the list fall into the wrong hands, prompting questions, investigations, unmaskings, expulsions. It was the linchpin of the entire operation: a hunk of cheese wrapped tightly in plastic.

Yawnee Valley cows ate Yawnee Valley grass from Yawnee Valley hills to make Yawnee Valley milk. Some Yawnee Valley milk became Yawnee Valley cheese, for sale to customers

of the Yawnee Valley Creamery, purveyor of twenty-seven
varieties including:

American
Baby Swiss
Blue
Brick
Cheddar (mild)
Cheddar (medium)
Cheddar (sharp)
Cheddar (extra-sharp)
Chèvre
Colby
Colby-Jack
Cream Cheese
Farmer Cheese
Fresh Jack
Lacy Swiss
Monterey Jack
Mozzarella
Muenster
Parmesan

Pepper Jack
Pinconning
Provolone
Quark
Swiss
Teleme
White Cheddar

If you counted, you know that's only twenty-six kinds of cheese. But you might be interested to know that Yawnee Valley is also one of only four places outside Germany to make Limburger cheese, which Miles Murphy had purchased this morning, and which is famous for smelling like feet.

"Aw man," said Miles, unwrapping the cheese. "It smells like feet."

"That's the whole point," said Niles.

"Yeah, but I can smell the feet," Miles said, "through the gas mask."

Niles shrugged. "I tried to tell you. Gas masks block poison, not smells."

Miles lifted the gas mask off his face. "OK. You win. I'll take a clothespin."

Niles smiled. "I only brought one."

Leave it to Niles Sparks to prank his pranking partner in the middle of a prank.

"Good one," said Miles.

"Thanks," said Niles.

Miles looked a little queasy. He stared at the cheese. "It's even worse than I thought." He took a deep breath and held it.

Miles and Niles nodded to each other.

Then they got down on the skateboards, flat on their backs, and rolled under a yellow hatchback that belonged to their principal, whose name was Principal Barkin, and who ate lunch at Danny's Diner at the same time every Sunday.

A good prank required a good goat, and a good goat was someone who deserved to be pranked. Good goats were despots and tyrants, preeners and egomaniacs. Principal Barkin was a great goat, having:

1) insisted, in speeches and on signs he pasted around the school, that his power as principal be respected by students;

2) thrown tantrums whenever that power was called into question, his face turning

purple any time he got angry (which was often);

3) canceled this year's theme days, citing "frivolity," including Wacky Hair Day, Mustache Day, and Backward Day, leaving only Pajama Day (a compromise brokered by the class president, and even then Barkin had driven a tough bargain: On Pajama Day, school would start fifteen minutes early, "since students would have no need to get dressed");

4) committed several other heinous acts, including all the stuff from the first book.

It took ninety-three seconds to coat the car's undercarriage with Limburger cheese, and so in less than two minutes they were standing next to the car again.

"How does it smell?" Niles asked.

"Terrible," Miles said.

They grinned. Miles held up two fingers. Niles did too. They touched their fingertips together. It was the secret handshake of the Terrible Two, perfect for celebrating a prank well done.

"Let's go," said Miles.

But Niles wasn't finished.

"Hold on."

He checked to be sure nobody was looking, then smeared a layer of cheese on the vents right below the car's windshield.

It was the masterstroke.

THE PRANKSTER'S OATH

ON MY HONOR I WILL DO MY BEST:
TO BE GOOD AT BEING BAD;
TO DISRUPT, BUT NOT DESTROY;
TO EMBARRASS THE DOUR AND
    AMUSE THE MERRY;
TO DEVOTE MY MIND TO JAPES,
    CAPERS, SHENANIGANS, AND
    MONKEY BUSINESS;
TO PROVE THE WORLD LOOKS BETTER
    TURNED UPSIDE DOWN;

FOR I AM A PRANKSTER.

SO BE IT.